ADAM'S CURSE

Erasmus Institute Books

ADAM'S CURSE

Reflections on Religion and Literature

DENIS DONOGHUE

University of Notre Dame Press

Notre Dame, Indiana

Manufactured in the United States of America

Designed by Wendy McMillen
Set in 11/13.5 Stone Print by Em Studio, Inc.
Printed by Sheridan Books, Inc.

Library of Congress Cataloging-in-Publication Data

Donoghue, Denis.
Adam's curse : reflections on religion and literature /
Denis Donoghue
p. m.—(Erasmus Institute books)
Includes bibliographical references and index.
ISBN 0-268-02009-4 (cloth : alk. paper)
1. English poetry—History and criticism.   2. Religious poetry,
English—History and criticism.   3. Christianity and literature—Great
Britain—History.   4. Christianity and literature—United States—History.
5. Religious poetry, American—History and criticism.   6. Christian poetry,
American—History and criticism.   7. Christian poetry, English—
History and criticism.   8. American poetry—History and
criticism.   9. Religion and literature.
I. Title.   II. Series.
PR508.R4 D66 2001
821.009'382—dc21   00-011708

∞ *This book is printed on acid-free paper.*

Again

FOR FRANCES

AND THE CHILDREN

CONTENTS

ACKNOWLEDGMENTS

I AM GRATEFUL TO JAMES TURNER AND NATHAN HATCH FOR inviting me to inaugurate the Erasmus Lectures at the University of Notre Dame in March and April 2000 and for giving me a free hand in choosing a theme. I would like to think that the lectures were at least compatible with the larger purposes of the Erasmus Institute. I am also grateful to Gary Gutting for his help in clarifying some of the issues I raised.

The period I spent at Notre Dame was much enhanced for me by the kindness of Robert Sullivan, Kathleen Sobieralski, and their colleagues at the Institute.

ADAM'S CURSE

ONE EVENING IN MAY 1902 W. B. YEATS TALKED TO MAUD GONNE and her sister Kathleen in a drawing room in Kensington while they looked at the moon rising. The theme was poetry, but it developed into a larger one, the difficulty of doing anything worthwhile. The evening is recalled in Yeats's poem "Adam's Curse." According to the poem, Yeats and Kathleen did most of the talking. He complained of the labor involved in writing a poem, the inevitable stitching and unstitching, and the need to make the poem seem in the end to transcend the difficulties and become "a moment's thought." Kathleen, bringing the issue close to home, said:

> 'To be born woman is to know—
> Although they do not talk of it at school—
> That we must labor to be beautiful.'

Yeats, with love on his mind and Maud Gonne beside him, said:

> 'It's certain there is no fine thing
> Since Adam's fall but needs much laboring.
> There have been lovers who thought love should be
> So much compounded of high courtesy
> That they would sigh and quote with learned looks
> Precedents out of beautiful old books;
> Yet now it seems an idle trade enough.'

Maud had good reason to stay silent. Yeats regarded her as his spiritual wife, and thought—or forced himself to believe—that there was an unbreakable bond between them. But it was a tiring relation, with no consummation in sight. He did not know the truth, that Maud had decided to become a Catholic and marry Major John McBride, an Irish hero of the Boer War. The poem does not record any words that passed between Yeats and Maud, but it recites what he would have said to her in private:

> I had a thought for no one's but your ears:
> That you were beautiful, and that I strove
> To love you in the old high way of love;
> That it had all seemed happy, and yet we'd grown
> As weary-hearted as that hollow moon.[1]

I I

I have called this inaugural series of Erasmus Lectures at the University of Notre Dame "Adam's Curse" because Yeats's poem points to my theme, the conditions that make any achievement difficult, the shadow that falls—as T. S. Eliot writes in "The Hollow Men"—between the potency and the existence, between the essence and the descent. The conditions include at various levels of reference the Fall of Man, categorical failure, loss, the limitations inscribed so insistently in human life that they seem to be in the nature of things, like death and weather. There is also, but not as a matter of course, the possibility of putting up with the conditions and turning them to some account.

I haven't approached the theme with an ambition to be comprehensive or even consecutive. I have chosen to produce a few samples or instances, in the hope that each will throw some light, however obliquely, on the theme. If a motto were needed to indicate the governing prejudice of the lectures, Coleridge's remark would be decisive:

> A FALL of some sort or other—the creation, as it were, of the non-absolute—is the fundamental postulate of the moral history of man.

Without this hypothesis, man is unintelligible; with it, every phenomenon is explicable. The mystery itself is too profound for human insight.[2]

But this consideration, true as I believe it to be, is too grand to be locally useful: if we attended to it as fully as it deserves, we would find ourselves appalled, silenced on every passing issue. A more modest theory of difficulty would be helpful.

Gabriel Josipovici has offered one in his *On Trust*. We live in an age of suspicion, as various writers from Stendhal to Nathalie Sarraute have maintained. Josipovici argues that what suspicion undermines is trust: trust in the world, in other people, in language, and in oneself. Homer and the writers of the Bible had a certain "lightness" because they trusted to their craft, an inherited body of skill and lore which they took up and practiced without being self-conscious in its possession. They did not worry, apparently, about language or suspect their instruments. They took the instruments on trust. But at some point—if we construe the matter historically—writers lapsed from that trust, or discovered that they could not take their craft or their traditions for granted. Josipovici equivocates between thinking of the issue historically and thinking of it categorically. In some parts of the book he presents Plato and St. Paul as adepts of suspicion. In other parts he seems to think that Shakespeare represents the point at which suspicion, in its bearing on human relations and on language, came to be defined. *A Midsummer Night's Dream* is based on trust, but *Hamlet*, *Othello*, the history plays, and the problem plays are oppressed by suspicion. The rival values meet in Iago's victory over Othello. Suspicion darkens the epiphanies of Wordsworth and Coleridge, and nearly paralyzes the creative impulse in Kafka and Beckett. "Nothing is granted to me," Kafka writes to Milena, "everything has to be earned, not only the present and the future, but the past too."[3]

The crucial proponents of suspicion in modern thought are Marx, Nietzsche, and Freud, who respectively troubled the common understanding of economics and politics, morality, and sexual practices. Josipovici adds Kierkegaard, mainly on the strength of the section of *Either/Or* called "The Ancient Tragical Motif as Reflected in the Modern." In that

section Kierkegaard distinguishes modern from ancient tragedy by refer-
ence to the higher degree of reflection in modern tragedy. "When the age
loses the tragic," he says, "it gains despair."[4]

> In ancient tragedy the sorrow is deeper, the pain less; in modern, the
> pain is greater, the sorrow less. Sorrow always contains something
> more substantial than pain. Pain always implies a reflection over suf-
> fering which sorrow does not know.[5]

Our age, according to Kierkegaard, "has lost all the substantial categories
of family, state, and race." As a consequence, there is no value to which an
individual may consign his sorrow or his guilt: the age "must leave the in-
dividual entirely to himself, so that in a stricter sense he becomes his own
creator, his guilt is consequently sin, his pain remorse; but this nullifies
the tragic."[6] In the second volume of *Either/Or* the speaker replies to the
aesthete of the first volume by associating the aesthetic life with despair
and claiming that it is only in the ethical life that despair gains its signifi-
cance and becomes "a metamorphosis."[7] But the movement from Greek
tragedy to modern despair is one instance of the suspicion that Josipovici
describes—suspicion that remembers the old objective values but will
not or cannot maintain them.

The equivocation in Josipovici's book between historical and categori-
cal approaches is not a defect: it leaves us wondering, usefully, whether
the movement from trust to suspicion, from craft to virtuosity, from sor-
row to pain, and from tragedy to despair is a matter of temperament—
Plato rather than Aristotle and Thucydides; Kafka and Beckett rather
than Proust—or attributable to historical forces. If it is a matter of tem-
perament, the causes have to be sought in each case and are likely to be
hard to find. If historical forces are in question, the likeliest ones are the
Reformation and the Enlightenment, the conjoined forces that offered
salvation—secular and temporal rather than in any strict sense reli-
gious—through the acquisition of knowledge and the power of knowl-
edge. Yeats wrote "Leda and the Swan" to express his conviction that
"after the individualist, demagogic movement, founded by Hobbes and
popularized by the Encyclopaedists and the French Revolution, we have a
soil so exhausted that it cannot grow that crop again for centuries."

"Nothing is now possible," he thought, "but some movement from above preceded by some violent annunciation."[8] We recognize in those sentences the clenched paradigm of Yeats's later poetry. But the Reformation, the Enlightenment, and the French Revolution also amounted to a violent annunciation, even if in the long run they settled agreeably enough for the comforts of bourgeois liberalism. Zeus's "shudder in the loins" in "Leda and the Swan" engendered more than "the broken wall, the burning roof and tower/And Agamemnon dead." It engendered a form of life consistent with Yeats's question about Leda:

> Being so caught up,
> So mastered by the brute blood of the air,
> Did she put on his knowledge with his power
> Before the indifferent beak could let her drop?[9]

Evidently she did, and the despair of which Kierkegaard speaks is the disappointment attendant upon the Enlightenment and its easy promise. In the chapter on Beckett, Josipovici says that *The Unnamable* turns upside down "the Kantian Enlightenment notion that as free beings we must speak what we think."[10] The Unnamable says, "Dear incomprehension, it's thanks to you I'll be myself in the end."[11]

There are many signs of disappointment with the Enlightenment. In one of these lectures I consider Levinas's *Otherwise than Being* as such a sign. The turn from first philosophy to politics and ethics—evident in Adorno, Habermas, Rorty, Cavell, and other philosophers—speaks to similar impulses. Josipovici hopes that it may still be possible to recover the old trust or animate a new form of it; if not, there can be no escape from suspicion.

III

Twenty-five years later, in "Among School Children," Yeats returned to the theme of Adam's curse, and imagined that it might be possible to take the harm out of labor by living as the natural world lives or by transforming labor into work or play and the joy of it:

Labour is blossoming or dancing where
The body is not bruised to pleasure soul,
Nor beauty born out of its own despair,
Nor blear-eyed wisdom out of midnight oil.[12]

In his early poems, Yeats often imagined pre-lapsarian states of being, free of time and—according to Joachim de Fiore's vision—free of law. "Adam's Curse" is one of the first poems in which he acknowledged the pressure of body, time, age, and death, considerations never absent from his later poems. The force of the grim, dragging words in "Adam's Curse"—"labor," "laboring," "strove," "trade," "hollow," and "weary-hearted"—incriminates nature and culture alike, darkens our sense of both. "Among School Children" is a revision of "Adam's Curse." In the later poem Yeats does not contemplate the world as it would be if Adam and Eve had not disobeyed God. For the moment, he is thinking of the possibilities that remain after Adam's sin, the *felix culpa*, and his expulsion from the garden. He is thinking of still-possible instances of *sprezzatura*, of "the old nonchalance of the hand," of poems that seem to be a moment's thought, and of beauty and wisdom that seem to be given by grace of nature. Josipovici points to similar possibilities even in the age of suspicion, most of them to be found in Beckett. He reveres Beckett, although in logic he should deplore his apparent starting point, capitulation to the aesthetics of suspicion. For Josipovici, *Molloy, Malone Dies, The Unnamable*, and *Endgame* together make the *felix culpa* of suspicion, not to be wished away. In "Among School Children" Yeats has not forgotten Adam's curse or the necessity of living by the sweat of one's brow, but he recognizes certain achievements that are still possible, and he finds them good. This is his version of the recovery of trust, of a mood in which such recovery seems possible.

Of course any reader may insist on a suspicious reading of "Among School Children." Paul de Man insists, in "Semiology and Rhetoric," and claims that while we are interpreting the question—"How can we know the dancer from the dance?"—it is impossible to decide between a rhetorical reading and a grammatical reading. A rhetorical reading of Yeats's line would take it as a celebration of the possibility of Unity of Being, the wondrous indistinguishability of dancer and dance. A grammatical reading would take it as saying "Please tell me, how *can* I know the dancer from the dance?" De Man professes that he is willing "to equate the rhetorical, figural potentiality of language with literature itself,"[13] but on this occasion he refuses to read the poem rhetorically, or to give such a reading any privilege. "Rhetoric radically suspends logic and opens up vertiginous possibilities of referential aberration."[14] So he submits Yeats's line, at least notionally, to the jurisdiction of logic and grammar, and refuses to be swayed by considerations of figure, image, rhythm, or other poetic attributes. His version of Deconstruction is—to use Paul Ricoeur's phrase—the hermeneutics of suspicion. He refuses to let rhetoric displace grammar.

I V

In *Genesis* God imposes three curses. First, on the serpent:

Because thou hast done this, thou art cursed above all cattle, and above every beast of the field; upon thy belly shalt thou go, and dust shalt thou eat all the days of thy life:

Then on the woman, not yet named Eve:

I will greatly multiply thy sorrow and thy conception; in sorrow thou shalt bring forth children; and thy desire shall be to thy husband, and he shall rule over thee.

Finally on Adam:

Because thou hast hearkened unto the voice of thy wife, and hast eaten of the tree, of which I commanded thee, saying, Thou shalt not eat of it: cursed is the ground for thy sake; in sorrow shalt thou eat of it all the days of thy life;

Thorns also and thistles shall it bring forth to thee; and thou shalt eat the herb of the field;

In the sweat of thy face shalt thou eat bread, till thou return unto the ground; for out of it wast thou taken: for dust thou art, and unto dust shalt thou return. (3:14–19)

The curses are appalling, such that Milton in *Paradise Lost* could hardly bear to recite them. He persuaded himself to repeat the curses on the serpent and on Adam vigorously enough, but he couldn't allow the woman to be afflicted with desire for her husband. So he makes her subjection a vague state, and permits us to think that it might be a social or economic imperative only:

> "Thy sorrow I will greatly multiply
> By thy conception; children thou shalt bring
> In sorrow forth, and to thy husband's will
> Thine shall submit, he over thee shall rule."[15]

We expected "bring forth" without any interruption between the two words, as it is in *Genesis*, but Milton has folded the sorrow within the experience of childbirth; just as the interruption of the sentence in "and to thy husband's will" commits the emphasis to "Thine" and "shall" and "over thee."

So the title of Yeats's "Adam's Curse" admits an irony. Maud Gonne is not subject to her spiritual husband; nor is she afflicted by any desire for him. It is a symbolic act on Yeats's part to make the conditions of subjection somewhat more general, more widely pervasive, bearing not only on love and sex but on art and beauty. Both women are beautiful, so their labors are blossoming. And the poet has written fine poems, the stitching and unstitching worthwhile. There will be another time for despair, stretching far beyond the present mood.

V

I have spoken of the conditions that make any achievement difficult, but I have not yet mentioned one of the most encompassing of those, the inadequacy of language. The sense of that inadequacy is acute in many of the writers I'll refer to, but it may help if I say a preliminary word or two about the issue. There are several feasible attitudes toward language. I will mention only three of them.

Some writers regard language, in the form of speech, as a redemptive gift, or at least as a protective possession. In "The Cool Web" Robert Graves writes:

> But we have speech, to chill the angry day,
> And speech, to dull the rose's cruel scent.
> We spell away the overhanging night,
> We spell away the soldiers and the fright.

It is difficult to claim, in our time, that speech spells away the soldiers and the fright. Some forms of speech, as in Hitler's Germany, mobilized the soldiers and set them to work in the death-camps. But Graves is prepared to claim that we would be in more hopeless plight if we gave up our trust in language, frail as it is:

> But if we let our tongues lose self-possession,
> Throwing off language and its watery clasp
> Before our death, instead of when death comes,
> Facing the wide glare of the children's day,
> Facing the rose, the dark sky, and the drums,
> We shall go mad no doubt and die that way.[16]

Presumably Graves means by language mainly grammar and syntax, or in speech the colloquial versions of them, the forces that make for community and perhaps even for conviviality, despite the worst that can be said.

But some writers are not to be appeased by that consideration. In the *Essay Concerning Human Understanding* Locke argues that lies, deceit, and seduction are inscribed in the figurative insistence of words. He thinks that language is rotten with eloquence. The figures of speech are designed to "insinuate wrong *ideas*, move the passions, and thereby mislead the judgment, and so indeed are perfect cheat."[17] People prefer to deceive and to be deceived rather than to live by clear ideas and perceptions. The obvious answer to Locke is that he lives by such a cut-back version of truth that he is bound to be dismayed by metaphors and other figures: he keeps pruning the tree because he's afraid to let it take its course.

A third attitude to language is that it's a blunt instrument but the best we have. Valéry complained that a poet, even in his most rarefied strivings, has to use the standard words and yet make them responsive to his vision, even if it is ineffable. He envied the composer who has at his disposal sounds and relations among sounds that have not been dulled on the streets. In "Little Gidding" T. S. Eliot has the "familiar compound ghost" say that "last year's words belong to last year's language/And next year's words await another voice." But within a few lines the ghost holds out a minor possibility:

> Since our concern was speech, and speech impelled us
>> To purify the dialect of the tribe
>> And urge the mind to aftersight and foresight, . . .[18]

Even if this purity is impossibly Mallarméan, the effort to achieve it is worthwhile: it stands for every impulse toward a better life; another theme, though a submerged one, in several of the writers I speak of.

But Valéry is of two minds in regard to language. He wants it to be responsive to writers, but not to capitulate to them. In *Degas Manet Morisot* he says that true artists are vexed by art in which the material fails to offer "any positive resistance."[19] An artist should have to work for his formal perfections, even if the working feels like its servile cousin, labor.

V I

Why "reflections on religion and literature"? Why religion; why literature; why, even more to the point, the pathos of "and," bringing into the same field of reference values that may not want to be familiarly associated? Each is a deviation, and increasingly a vagabond, a nomad, a critic. Religion deviates from the material ways of the world. Literature deviates from the orders of economics, law, and rationality, even though it is obliged to them and could not exist without the political economy it affects to deride. And "and" deviates from the old consanguinities that made the assertion of "and" unnecessary. No wonder the values are hated, all three.

God without Thunder

On July 4, 1929, the poet and critic John Crowe Ransom wrote to his friend Allen Tate to congratulate him on an essay, "The Fallacy of Humanism," he had recently published in T. S. Eliot's journal *The Criterion*. Ransom agreed with Tate that religion is prior to politics, economics, or any other secular discipline. Inclined to add a few footnotes to Tate's essay, he continued:

> The fear of the Lord is the beginning of wisdom; a big beginning, but only a beginning of which the end is the love of the Lord. Substitute nature for the Lord and he won't feel aggrieved. The Jews knew all about that in their Old Testament; the New Testament was a temptation which the soft-headed Western World couldn't resist; in the N. T. it seems (to the soft-headed W. W.) that the love of the Lord is the beginning of wisdom, and it's the kind of love a world bears to a faithful slave-population, or public service that never sleeps; better, the kind a scientist bears to the gentle, tractable elements in his testtubes, which so gladly yield him of their secrets, and work for him. The N. T. has been a failure & a backset as a religious myth; not its own fault, as I think, but nevertheless a failure; it's hurt us.[1]

Before I comment on that passage, I should say that Ransom was not a systematic or otherwise rigorous thinker. He was a poet, a minor one no doubt, but one of the best in that honorable category. In his essays he tended to exhaust his conviction of the moment in the labor of express-ing it. Within no time, or after a brief interval, he was ready to move on to new avowals and almost to deny that he had ever thought otherwise. So I shall be speaking of his religious convictions only as I find them in 1929 and for a few months thereafter, and I shall be concentrating on their representative value. Surveying his career as a whole, I should report that Ransom gradually lost his arduous religious faith and devoted his en-ergy to aesthetics and the theory of poetry. I don't know whether he aban-doned his religious convictions because he thought they had no future in the world or because they did not survive his changes of heart and mind. In the end and perhaps to some degree because of the persuasive powers exerted by Santayana and Dewey, he became some kind of naturalist, secularist, or Unitarian.

That change could have been foreseen in his letter to Tate. If you say "Substitute nature for the Lord and he won't feel aggrieved," you are offer-ing a program good enough for certain kinds of poetry but not for a de-manding religion. The formula is, in effect, Spinoza's: *Deus sive natura*. God is the first name of the one substance whose other name is Nature. Like Spinoza, Ransom seems to be claiming that God is identical with the creative, self-sustaining power at work in the natural world, *natura natu-rans*. If you took the two parts of Spinoza's formula separately, you could think of God as absolute power at one with his infinite attributes; or you could revel in the plenitude of Nature and find no need to invoke God at all. Under that second article, Spinoza, as Coleridge said, "withdraws God from the universe."[2] Under the first, you could think of God as infinite power, but not as any other quality. Ransom elaborated the second or pan-theistic article in a later book, *The World's Body*, where he argued that a poet's love of the natural world in its variety and richness is enough.

But in 1929 he emphasized the first article and insisted on God's power as if he were intent on fulfilling Spinoza's concept of *unica substan-tia*. God has no purpose or desires for the world. It follows that the atti-tude I should take to God is one of awe or fear, in consideration of the fact that God's being is absolutely independent of mine. I must not com-mit what Tillich called "the sin of religion" by identifying God's will with my own. In 1929 Ransom was writing a book which he thought of calling *Giants for Gods*. That title didn't survive: the book was published the following year as *God without Thunder*. In the letter to Allen Tate, Ransom gave the gist of it with a flurry of assertions:

> The point is that so many myth-systems (doubtless all of them) have contained myths (*many* in the Greek system) of giants, or earth-born (super-man in Nietzsche's myth), who were not Gods but only demi-Gods, yet *thought* they were Gods and behaved themselves accordingly. Prometheus, for example, whom the Greeks with all their intellectualism could not quite endorse. . . . Satan is the Hebrew Prometheus and so conceived in Milton's *P[aradise] L[ost]*—he is *Lucifer* the spirit of the Renaissance, the Zeitgeist of Milton's own age of science, very *boldly* displayed and only rejected after a proper hesitation. But then *Jesus* is *Lucifer* again; all the Saviors in the myths are Giants, *and the problem is in what sense they can save, and for what purpose they are to be worshipped*. Of course they are all earth-born, or half-human and half-god; the whole matter of the myth is to ask & determine the question, what is *man's* destiny, what is his proper relation to the God of nature? The function of Jesus in setting up as a Giant was to *decline* to set up as a God. But he may have wavered in his purpose; or the myth-makers in theirs, if you prefer. So the Western world raised this Giant to God, better than HOMOI-OUSION, in fact HOMO-OUSION; little by little the God of the Jews has been whittled down into the Spirit of Science, or the Spirit of Love, or the Spirit of Rotary; *and now religion is not religion at all, but a purely secular experience, like Y. M. C. A. and Boy Scouts*. Humanism in religion means pretending that Man is God.[3]

Ransom's bit of Greek says that the Western world turned Jesus into God, made him more than "of like substance" to God, in fact "of the same substance."

I haven't seen Tate's reply to Ransom's letter, if he made one that has survived, but many years later in an essay he published after Ransom's death, he noted that Ransom had "repudiated the liturgical Christianity advocated in *God without Thunder*." I don't know the evidence for this claim, but it doesn't surprise me. "I still agree with the main argument of that book," Tate maintained, "that is, I don't see how Christianity can survive as a humanistic doctrine: there must be a theistic God, apodeictic and menacing as well as merciful."[4]

God without Thunder has the subtitle *An Unorthodox Defense of Orthodoxy,* but it is a backhanded defense if one at all. By orthodoxy Ransom evidently meant the Eastern church from which the Western churches had lapsed. In a preface to the book, he says: "The predicament of religionists today may be stated as follows: they have not much more to lose." By religion he means "a body of doctrine concerning God and man." It is "an order of experience under which we indulge the compound attitude of fear, respect, enjoyment, and love for the external nature in the midst of which we are forced to live. We were born of earth—why should we spurn it?"[5] You can see that he is taking each part of Spinoza's formula separately. The device would satisfy a poet, but it might not be enough for a religionist. Ransom continues:

> But the doctrine which defines God, and man's relation to God, is really a doctrine which tries to define the intention of the universe, and man's proper portion within this universe.[6]

Ransom's more clamorous argument is that the Western churches— for brevity, we may call them Rome and Canterbury—have ignored the God of the Old Testament in favor of Jesus. They have established Jesus as God. The God of the Old Testament "*is the author of evil as well as good, and one can never be sure which of the two is coming next.*" But Rome and Canterbury want God to be "wholly benevolent, and ethical after the humane definition." What will they do about evil? They will do nothing about it, they will pretend that it is not there:

> They are not necessarily Christian Scientists in the technical sense, for they do acknowledge some evil, of a kind which is now or prospectively curable by the secular sciences. But they are virtually Christian Scientists so far as they gloze the existence of incurable evil. They represent evil in general as a temporary, incidental, negligible, and slightly uncomfortable phenomenon, which hardly deserves an entry in the theological ledger. They have no God for it.[7]

Later, Ransom gives a more formal and more astringent account of the matter:

> As I understand the myth of the Garden of Eden, it meant to express something substantially like this: Satan is the Demigod, the Prometheus, the Spirit of Secular Science, who would like to set up falsely as the God, the Ruler of the Universe—beware of him.
>
> And as I understand the myth of Christ, it meant: Christ also is the Demigod, the Man-God, who represents the highest human development—but observe how he refuses to try to be the God; believe on him in the light of his self-confessed limitations.
>
> Satan was the Pretender, the Archangel who aspired. Christ was the Son who had no intentions upon his Father's throne. So the role of Christ was of a nobility almost unparalleled in the lore of myths: *to be the Demigod who refused to set up as the God.*
>
> But by an exquisite irony the disciples of Christ have disobeyed his admonitions, forgotten his limits, and made him assume the throne after all—where he sits now quite incompetent to rule over the dominions of another. . . .
>
> Christ was a subordinate figure in the early Christian Godhead. He is now become, or at least he is rapidly becoming, the whole Godhead.[8]

Ransom does not say how this has come about, or on what authority. My own sense of the matter is that those Christians who couldn't bear to base their religion on awe and fear resorted to that episode in the Gospel according to John in which Philip had the temerity to ask Christ: "Lord, shew us the Father, and it sufficeth us." Jesus, obviously exasperated, answered:

> Have I been so long time with you, and yet hast thou not known me, Philip? He that hath seen me hath seen the Father; and how sayest thou then, Shew us the Father?
>
> Believest thou not that I am in the Father, and the Father in me? The words that I speak unto you I speak not of myself: but the Father that dwellest in me, he doeth the works. (14:8–10)

If you wanted to for other reasons, you might take Christ as telling Philip that he need not concern himself much with the Father.

Ransom held, as you might expect, that in Rome and Canterbury "there is hardly any such thing as a *theology*, in the Western sense of a system of religious concepts, which has ever successfully defined, ordered, and assimilated all the great ghosts which throng that brief document, the New Testament":

> Its wealth exceeds our grasp, and it is because the theologians have failed so badly—though sometimes honestly and charmingly—in this task, that there is always fresh work for private initiative.[9]

Ransom doesn't quite say—he hardly needs to—that theology has fallen to psychology and that most of the sermons we hear in church are merely psychology in its popular and facile forms. The Eucharist remains, a celebration of giving-and-receiving, the Last Supper, but it is regularly surrounded by easy talk.

It is time to make some observations, beginning with this one. Ransom is susceptible to the Arian heresy; he does not take seriously the consubstantiality of the three persons in God. Perhaps he regarded as decisive the fact that the Hebrew Bible does not contain a doctrine of the Trinity. Nor does the New Testament, if we read it strictly. It is true that John's Gospel says (1:1) "In the beginning was the Word, and the Word was with God, and the Word was God," and that John also has Jesus say (10:30): "I and my Father are one." But John also has Jesus say (14:28) "My Father is greater than I," a statement the Arians fastened on. In the event it took nearly three hundred years after the death of Christ for an orthodox theology of the Trinity to develop. God is one nature, three persons: in Augustine's phrase, *Tres et Unus*. Or in Rahner's terms: "God is 'threefold', through His three manners of subsisting."[10] Tertullian formulated a trinitarian theology that presented the three persons as a plurality in God. But Arius denied that Christ was fully divine, and he had enough followers to make a scandal: so the Council of Nicaea in 325 taught that Christ is *homoousis*, of the same substance with God, not merely of like substance. In 381 the Council of Constantinople affirmed the divinity of the Holy Spirit. Augustine took as his starting point, in the *De Trinitate*,

the one divine substance which the three persons share. Boethius eluci-
dated the nature of 'person' in these formulations as "individual sub-
stance of a rational nature." Aquinas's version is: "that which subsists
distinctly (in a rational nature)." The crucial consideration is to retain the
concept of three 'persons' without thinking of them as three spiritual
centers of activity. As Rahner says, there are not three consciousnesses,
"there is only one real consciousness in God, which is shared by Father,
Son, and Spirit, by each in his own proper way."[11] The single 'person' in
God is "God as existing and meeting us in this determined distinct man-
ner of subsisting."[12] Each divine person exists by relation to the other
two, and each fully possesses the divine substance. Ransom seems to ac-
cept none of this. He evidently believes that God the Father is the sole
independent power, and that Jesus is subordinate, as a Demigod is sub-
ordinate to the God. Ransom thinks of the two as separate entities. He
needs to do this, if he is to denounce Rome and Canterbury for setting up
a God in their own sweet, kindly image.

Ransom does not ignore the Trinity, but he has a strange notion of it.
He holds that the Holy Ghost was added to Father and Son to complete
the fullness of God: it was necessary to make some formal acknowledg-
ment of the awful, unpredictable, and arbitrary features of God the
Father. "The Father is our father, and the Son is ourselves." The Holy
Ghost represents the demonic qualifications:

> The inscrutable and awful God of the Jews, whose name was the inef-
> fable Tetragram, was being reduced to a Father, who had acknowl-
> edged man as his son and heir, and upon whose goodness man was
> quite ready to presume. But the rational and humane essence which
> he had imparted through the act of paternity, and which he and man
> therefore shared in common, had not exhausted his nature, nor de-
> fined the entire process by which he governed his universe. There
> was also an essence, an exceedingly energetic one, which was irra-
> tional and contingent, for all that human reason could do to compass
> it, and either indifferent or cruel, for all that it seemed to sympathize
> with human desires. So the Holy Ghost was the ghost who came to
> bear witness of God in his fullness.[13]

The collapse of modern belief in the Holy Ghost is yet another sign, Ransom claims, of our determination to think of God in agreeable terms, as God without thunder.

It is hard to challenge this last claim. Rahner complains, in his book on the Trinity, that Christians have become, in their practical lives, "monotheist." "Should the doctrine of the Trinity have to be dropped as false," he says, "the major part of religious literature could well remain virtually unchanged."[14] Ransom extends the case to include the whole range of religion in the modern world. Religionists, as he calls them, have accepted their defeat and made genial terms with their former enemies. Ransom speaks of the two camps as fraternizing with each other:

> And that is . . . the way in which their hostilities are becoming a mere formality, while the religionists are coming gradually to a perfect understanding with the anti-religionists in which they are the losers and the anti-religionists are the winners. The priests themselves have lost heart and are not handing on the priestly tradition. They have in effect come to this arrangement with the naturalists: "If you will leave us the name and honor of our Gods, we will surrender to you their powers and see that you are not interfered with in your naturalism and your secularism."
>
> That is the intent of the new theology, which makes Christ supreme over all other Gods. For Christ is the spirit of the scientific and ethical secularism of the West.[15]

Ransom found this conclusion inevitable, and it was, given that he had separated God the Father from God the Son and identified the Son with our own worldly purposes: in the modern world, scientific and ethical secularism is widely regarded as the highest form of ourselves.

So Ransom comes to a foreseeable set of admonitions, which he conveys with the emphasis of italics:

> *With whatever religious institution a modern man may be connected, let him try to turn it back towards orthodoxy.*
>
> *Let him insist on a virile and concrete God, and accept no Principle as a substitute.*

Let him restore to God the thunder.

Let him resist the usurpation of the Godhead by the soft modern version of the Christ, and try to keep the Christ for what he professed to be: the Demigod who came to do honor to the God.[16]

I I

At this point, or soon, I should put the question: what would it mean, given the current state of our theologies, to obey Ransom's admonition and restore to God the thunder? But before I do so, I want to turn from one attack on the Christian churches to another one far more lurid. I will treat this one only for its representative value, even if it seems to be remarkably offensive. Ransom's rebuke came from within the Church, and was uttered more in disappointment than in rage. William Empson's came from outside. He hated Christianity all his life, and thought himself a companion of Gibbon, Shelley, and Blake in that hatred. In his several books he took every opportunity to denounce Christianity, but he saved most of his venom for *Milton's God* (1961). In a few respects Empson agreed with Ransom, but he otherwise interpreted the evidence toward the opposite conclusion.

Empson hated Christianity because he hated God the Father. He believed that Christianity was founded on sacrifice, blood-lust, and "torture-worship," not on the Incarnation but on the Crucifixion. He construed God the Father as vindictive, arbitrary, a monster raging for blood. "The Christian God the Father, the God of Tertullian, Augustine and Aquinas, is the wickedest thing yet invented by the black heart of man."[17] Empson interpreted the Bible and Milton's *Paradise Lost* in that spirit. When he wanted some historical evidence, he found it mainly in Gibbon's *Decline and Fall of the Roman Empire*, especially in the chapters that recite the murderous dealings of Catholics, Arians, Sabellians, and other groups in the fourth century in Alexandria. But Empson had a more immediate incentive. He was appalled by the spread of neo-Christianity, as he called it, among modern literary critics who read poems and novels within a supposedly Christian tradition they do not even think of criticizing.

I don't propose to go through *Milton's God* or review Empson's interpretation of Milton's poem. For the sake of clarity I will confine myself to the last chapter of the book, called "Christianity," where Empson makes his most elaborate speech for the prosecution. He concentrates on three claims. The first is that Christianity, among the great religions, was the only one that insisted on dragging back "the Neolithic craving for human sacrifice into its basic structure."[18] God's sacrifice of his son was unnecessary and worked merely to the gratification of the sacrificer:

> When the Christian God sacrifices his Son, he can hardly be envisaged as acting under necessity because it appears that the Son can bribe him by the offer; that is why the Father is a very bad example to imitate.[19]

The second charge has to do with the Trinity. "A Christian reader," Empson says, "will be feeling that there is an obvious and decisive answer to such talk in the doctrine of the Trinity":

> The Father is in some sense identical with the Son, therefore the story means that God mysteriously sacrificed himself on behalf of mankind; because he so loved the world. He is thus infinitely above these stupid accusations. This doctrine, one can readily believe, was of crucial importance in shoring up the structure enough to make intelligent men with good feelings trust it. For the followers of Jesus to start murdering and torturing soon after they got power (e.g. Gibbon, Chap. 21 at n. 157) was ludicrous, but at least they needed to settle the Arian controversy as they did.[20]

In the revised edition Empson adds a note to say that Milton's poem "makes the Son and the Father about as unidentical as a terrier and a camel."[21] There is no talk of Donne's "three-personed God." Milton may or may not have been an Arian when he wrote the poem: "he might decide afterwards that what his imagination had produced amounted to being an Arian."[22] The order of events is not important, but it leads to Empson's third claim:

> Perhaps then the trouble with Milton's God in *Paradise Lost* is simply Milton's Arianism; his God is patently sacrificing someone else for a

political programme, whether his own Son or ourselves. But it seems to me that Milton was merely being honest there, because Christians can seldom avoid regarding the Son and the Father as he presents them.[23]

"I have thus to conclude," Empson reports, "that the Doctrine of the Trinity is a means of deceiving good men into accepting evil; it is the double-talk by which Christians hide from themselves the insane wickedness of their God."[24] "One can hardly discuss," he adds, "whether a man believes this doctrine, because it is merely a thing which his mind can be induced to do." The fact that Milton left the doctrine out of his poem without attracting unwelcome attention to the omission for over a hundred years proves, according to Empson, that the doctrine lies very lightly on the minds of most Christians.[25]

Empson apparently believed that Christians could give only notional assent rather than real assent to the doctrine of the Trinity. I take this distinction from the *Essay in Aid of a Grammar of Assent,* where Newman argues that it marks the difference between a belief that affects one's conduct and one that doesn't. He maintains that the doctrine of the Trinity can indeed be embraced with a real assent, but he thinks that the theological examination of the doctrine—involving such terms as substance, essence, existence, form, subsistence, and circumincession—commands only a notional assent. Empson argues that as soon as religionists start thinking about the Trinity, they have to try to visualize the three persons, and the doctrine of consubstantiality breaks down. Empson has no qualms about using the word 'person' in its ordinary human sense; he ignores the theology. He takes it for granted that the faithful think of God the Father in his imperious bearing; even if, like Ransom in *God without Thunder,* they deem awe or fear of Him to be the beginning of wisdom, and love of him the end. That's an entirely workable program, by the way. I started out in awe of my father, went on to revere him, and ended by loving him in a style that never presumed on intimacy. Empson would say: "that's well enough, but your father was not the monster of vindictiveness and whimsicality that God the Father was." Whatever image of God the Father Christians might have, they would have no problem with the image of Jesus: he could be severe, and make startling demands on his flock, but he was humane and selfless on their behalf. But again, you have only to keep turning the Bible into images and the Arian damage is done. The fact that you can't imagine what the Holy Ghost looks like means that, in practice, you ignore this third person, as Empson claims and Rahner ruefully concedes.

But the most fundamental problem arises not from the Arian heresy but from the nature of language and especially from the nature of narrative. It is possible to think about consubstantiality, and even to discuss it, as Augustine did, but you can't give it a narrative form without losing the whole doctrine. It is a prejudice of narrative form to turn entities into people, or semblances of people. Even an omniscient narrator becomes a person, someone you could think of interrogating. The authors of the Bible and *Paradise Lost* are Arians not necessarily for theological reasons but for narrative reasons: as soon as they make God speak, they turn him into a person in the ordinary untheological sense. In speech, God is forced to give up the singularity of His silence and to move into a human world of discourse. There are no special words for God which can express the divinity without changing God into a man. There are no words for the supernatural, the angelic, or the demonic. In *Paradise Lost*, as soon as Raphael speaks, he becomes a historian. When God speaks, he becomes an emperor. There are no words for Lucifer till he becomes Satan, and then he becomes merely human, exhibiting only human attributes—false pride, envy, self-delusion. Even as the Serpent, he is human. There is no help for it, it is the insistence of narrative. Give a snake a voice, and he becomes a devious, coiling man. Even without speaking, God becomes a man by appearing to listen, as in Hopkins's "The Wreck of the Deutschland" and the last sonnets. Prayer has the same effect, which explains why Christians petition God to send relief, rain, or domestic happiness, and continue to pray even when the first prayers have yielded no response. A semblance of a relation has been enacted. Narration commits the relation to further disclosures by making it submit to conditions of voice, body, and time. For narrative reasons, Milton had to distinguish God the Father from the Son: his poem is an epic, which requires some degree of differentiation among the personages. As a result, readers of the poem can't help turning it into a novel or a failed neo-Shakespearean tragedy, once they start talking about its characters. The only way they could avoid doing so would be by turning it into a ballet of abstract principles. Kenneth Burke goes far in this direction in his *Rhetoric of Religion*, by searching for logical and linguistic principles at work behind the characters of *Genesis* and Augustine's *Confessions*. His justification for doing so is his decision to develop the idea of *logos* into a theory of the Word, which he calls a *logology*.

Similarly, in "Notes toward a Supreme Fiction," starting with the title, Wallace Stevens replaces theology with fiction, reduces God to the human imagination before trying to make that divine, and asks readers to perceive "the idea/Of this invention, this invented world" before perceiving the world itself:

> You must become an ignorant man again
> And see the sun again with an ignorant eye
> And see it clearly in the idea of it.[26]

Further, he says, you are not to ask who made this sun or to "suppose an inventing mind as source/Of this idea" or "for that mind compose/A voluminous master folded in his fire." Besides:

> Phoebus is dead, ephebe. But Phoebus was
> A name for something that never could be named.[27]

Named, Phoebus became something else; or, as I would say in the present context, Phoebus became human by being made to take on a name and, worse still, to speak. Language is a changer of natures, it changes every nature into human nature. God has to put up with the indignity.

III

What would be entailed by restoring to God the thunder? Perhaps Ransom had in view the thoughts and images that occurred to the young Stephen Dedalus the day after he listened to the sermon at Belvedere on the four last things: death, judgment, hell, and heaven. The Catholic version of the voluminous master folded in his fire suffuses Stephen's mind and takes command of his voice:

> And lo the supreme judge is coming! No longer the lowly Lamb of God, no longer the meek Jesus of Nazareth, no longer the Man of Sorrows, no longer the Good Shepherd, He is seen now coming upon the clouds, in great power and majesty, attended by nine choirs of angels, angels and archangels, principalities, powers and virtues, thrones and dominations, cherubim and seraphim, God Omnipotent, God Everlasting. He speaks: and His voice is heard even at the farthest limits of space, even in the bottomless abyss. Supreme Judge, from His sentence there will be and can be no appeal. He calls the just to His side bidding them enter into the kingdom, the eternity of bliss prepared for them. The unjust He casts from Him, crying in His offended majesty: *Depart from me, ye cursed, into everlasting fire which was prepared for the devil and his angels.*[28]

Or perhaps, Father Mapple's sermon in chapter 9 of *Moby-Dick*, which moves from woe to delight, lies closer to Ransom's home:

> Woe to him who seeks to please rather than to appal! Woe to him whose good name is more to him than goodness! Woe to him who, in this world, courts not dishonor! . . . Delight,—top-gallant delight is to him, who acknowledges no law or lord, but the Lord his God, and is only a patriot to heaven. . . . And eternal delight and deliciousness will be his, who coming to lay him down, can say with his final breath—O Father!—chiefly known to me by Thy rod—mortal or immortal, here I die. I have striven to be Thine, more than to be this world's, or mine own. Yet this is nothing; I leave eternity to Thee; for what is man that he should live out the lifetime of his God?[29]

I'm sure that Ransom wanted to have the thunder include such sounds as those.

But he would also have wanted corresponding sounds within. I think he would have smiled somewhat ruefully to hear the sacrament of Confession, in Roman Catholic churches, hushed to Reconciliation, and sin softened to "those respects in which we have failed in the love of God and our neighbours." But the sacraments have survived, and the observances of Advent, Christmas, Lent, Holy Week, and Easter. Ransom might be content if we were to read our sacred texts more exactingly than we usually do, and let sharper images inhabit our minds. In *God without Thunder* he indicates how we might read the Book of Job.

Ransom regarded the Book of Job as "the purest single work of theology" in the Jewish Scriptures: it is there, he says, "that I would concentrate the 'wisdom of the Old Testament'," presumably because the beginning of that wisdom is fear. It is strange, then, that he does not comment on the beginning of the story where God in effect proposes to make a wager with Satan, that Job's probity and his fear of God will survive every stress that may be put upon them. A psychological interpretation, as in Jung's *Answer to Job*, does not work in God's favor. He appears whimsical and callous in his readiness to have Job suffer for no reason. Perhaps the wager is just a device to get the story started: it is used in that way in *Measure for Measure*. Ransom's commentary begins with Job's comforters:

> The friends of Job, as philosophers, are not equal to the task of confessing that moral order and world order are not two names for the same thing. They have made God good in their peculiar human sense, and if Job is in distress they tell him it is because he has sinned, since God would never do anything that wasn't 'right.' But Job is intellectually an honest man and he denies the charge. It is not an instance where the punishment is proportionate to the crime and, ethically, Job's sufferings are perfectly unaccountable. The debate is extremely full and competent. The superior young Buzite man enters it after a while, and is like John the Baptist preparing the way for the Son of God: for at last, after proper preparation, God himself speaks magnificently out of the whirlwind:
>
>> Hast thou entered into the springs of the sea? or hast thou walked in the search of the depth?
>>
>> Have the gates of death been opened unto thee? or hast thou seen the doors of the shadow of death?
>>
>> Hast thou perceived the breadth of the earth? declare if thou knowest it all.

Ransom emphasizes that God's order of discourse is entirely different from Job's and that God makes no effort to reduce the difference:

> God recounts his powers and his works uncompromisingly, as powers and works which are on another foundation than the ethical and scientific order of Job's mind. He has not bargained with Job, he has never acknowledged any responsibility for making himself intelligible or amenable to Job, and Job, becoming smaller and smaller, at length testifies:
>
>> I know that thou canst do everything, and that no thought can be withholden from thee.
>>
>> Who is he that hideth counsel without knowledge? therefore have I uttered that I understood not; things too wonderful for me, which I knew not.
>>
>> Hear, I beseech thee, and I will speak: I will demand of thee, and declare thou unto me.
>>
>> I have heard of thee by the hearing of the ear: but now mine eye seeth thee.
>>
>> Wherefore I abhor myself, and repent in dust and ashes.

Ransom interprets this passage as "the climax of Job's religious experience," but he doesn't comment further on it. I assume he means that Job has given up any expectations that arise from the ethical order and has reverted to the mode of fear. He goes in fear of God and does not even complain of being harshly treated. He seems to accept that the difference between the ethical order and the divine order is absolute.

In Robert Frost's "A Masque of Reason," God returns after a thousand years to thank Job for helping him to establish the principle that "There's no connexion man can reason out/Between his just deserts and what he gets":

> Too long I've owed you this apology
> For the apparently unmeaning sorrow
> You were afflicted with in those old days.
> But it was of the essence of the trial

You shouldn't understand it at the time.
It had to seem unmeaning to have meaning.
And it came out all right. I have no doubt
You realize by now the part you played
To stultify the Deuteronomist
And change the tenor of religious thought.
My thanks are to you for releasing me
From moral bondage to the human race.[30]

Frost's sense of the story is close to Ransom's: there must be no coming to terms, even in an apology delayed a thousand years. Ransom wants the story to end with Job's last short speech, and he dissociates himself from the Epilogue. "I pass over as an unworthy anti-climax," he says, "the epilogue in which God, who has thus humbled the pride of Job, relieves his sufferings and gives him twice as much of worldly prosperity as he has had before. This is somebody's 'happy ending' which spoils a tragedy."[31] Ransom's account of the Book is quite different from the standard one, according to which—as in the *New American Bible*—Job "recovers his attitude of humility and trust in God, which is deepened now and strengthened by his experience of suffering."[32] Other commentaries emphasize that while Job has heard of God by word of mouth, now "God has deigned to let himself be found by Job."[33]

   Gathering these motifs together: I appreciate how reluctant many Christians are to establish their religion on awe and fear of God, even if it is a stance that leads to love in the end. They don't want to think of themselves as frightenable. Why not go to love directly, they say, and make religion a companionable preoccupation? Besides, what thunder can we restore to God? He can hardly threaten us with destruction mightier than we are accomplishing from our own resources: can anything worse happen than hatred, disease, starvation, napalm, and genocide? Still, I would like to see the primacy of theology and doctrine established, and the commonplaces of psychology displaced, sent back where they belong. I concede that Ransom, too, becomes a psychologist of religion in his dealings with God the Father, even if the psychology he practices is a grim one. It is hard to stick to theology. But I recall that when I was a boy in the Christian Brothers School in Newry, I learned more of Catholicism from a prescribed book called *Apologetics and Catholic Doctrine* than from any other source. A few years later I relieved the strictures of that book—or took up more literary severities—by reading Mauriac's *God and Mammon* and Bernanos's *Diary of a Country Priest*. It seems a long time ago, and it is. Maybe it is too late for thunder, but I think our priests would do well to elucidate the sacred texts for us and not to transcend the hard sayings. It is inevitable that we read the Old Testament in a grim spirit; it makes any genial reading seem worthless.

But the New Testament is not all sweetness, light, and geniality. One way of restoring to God the thunder would entail reading the New Testament with a conviction that its tones have not been entirely softened by comparison with the Old. Priests should tell us what they think Christ meant by saying, in Matthew 10:34: "Think not that I am come to send peace on earth: I came, not to send peace but a sword." Is it enough to say, as the *New Jerome Biblical Commentary* says, that "the sword is not to be understood as implying a zealotic uprising but as a regrettable side effect of tension and division resulting from the uncompromising proclamation of the kingdom. Elsewhere Jesus declares peacemakers blessed."[34] It is implausible to think of a sword as a side effect. In Luke (12:49) Jesus says: "I am come to send fire on the earth; and what will I, if it be already kindled?" And in Luke (14:26) he says: "If any man come to me, and hate not his father, and mother, and wife, and children, and brethren, and sisters, yea, and his own life also, he cannot be my disciple." As a gloss on *hate* the *New Jerome Biblical Commentary* merely says: "The total commitment Jesus demands of his disciples is stated starkly."[35] And why precisely are the children of darkness wiser in their generation than the children of light?

Perhaps we hear the thunder of God the Father most clearly—most terrifyingly—in Paul's Epistle to the Philippians (2.12): "Wherefore, my beloved, as ye have always obeyed, not as in my presence only, but now much more in my absence, work out your own salvation with fear and trembling." Ransom would want to hear our priests meditate on that absenting phrase. He would want to restore to God the thunder if only because otherwise we assimilate God to ourselves and think our purposes are endorsed by Him.

T H R E E

Church and World

J. Leslie Houlden has speculated:

> Suppose no Christianity, no Church, Jesus just lives and then is exe-
> cuted. All we should know of him (and who would bother to look?)
> is the brief but pleasing obituary in Josephus, the Jewish historian
> of the late first century. But there is Christianity, and there is the
> Church.[1]

It is clear that Christ intended a church and that he founded one to the
extent of designating Peter the rock on which it would be built and the
apostles the instruments of its kinship, succession, and authority. But
Peter was not a rock and the apostles and other witnesses were soon too
dispersed to amount to an *ecclesia*. For many years after Christ's death
there were several loose groups holding different beliefs, nomadic vision-
aries clutching various secret gospels and poems. But there was no
church. It was entirely possible that the Judaic religion rather than Chris-
tianity would become a world religion. It was only less possible that some
other group would seize the day. Christianity was once a schism, as Mil-
ton noted in *Areopagitica*. It is still to me remarkable that a church came
into being and that it survived and grew in that character. Hopkins main-
tained, in a sermon, that Christ "reasoned and planned and invented by
acts of his own human genius, genius made perfect by wisdom of its
own, not the divine wisdom only," and that one proof of his genius and

29

wisdom was the Catholic Church, "its ranks and constitution, its rites and sacraments."[2] To survive as a religion, if Durkheim is right, Christianity had to become a church. There has never been a religion without a church. There have been magical practices and cults, but these lack the social and communal identity that makes a religion. "A Church," as Durkheim says, "is not a fraternity of priests; it is a moral community formed by all the believers in a single faith, laymen as well as priests." "A religion," he continues, "is a unified system of beliefs and practices relative to sacred things, that is to say, things set apart and forbidden—beliefs and practices which unite into one single moral community called a Church all those who adhere to them."[3] In that sense, there was no Christian Church till the end of the second century. At that stage you were deemed to be a Christian, a member of the Church, if you believed that Christ was the son of God and that he lived a palpable life, was crucified, and rose bodily from the dead. If you did not hold those beliefs but still claimed to be a Christian, you were a heretic. Christianity was a story, and the Church's main work was to guard the story and develop sacraments and rituals to correlate the sacred events with the normal events of one's life. That was the Church's way of making sense while retaining the mysteries. The Eucharist remembers the Last Supper and observes the social value of meals eaten in common. Doctrines of the Church issue from a narrative rather than a discursive relation to the life of Christ.

What I find astonishing is that the Christian Church defeated the heretics not by offering a simpler structure of belief but by insisting on a more difficult one. It is hardly permissible to speak these days of the Gnostics. Some scholars have argued that their existence is so spectral that the very name of Gnosticism should be discarded.[4] But there were undoubtedly people, whether we call them Gnostics or not, who refused to believe that Christ was the son of God or that he rose bodily from the dead. The Christ they recognized spoke not of sin, repentance, and redemption but of illusion and enlightenment. The so-called Gnostics believed that self-knowledge and knowledge of God are one and the same: that is why they are called Gnostics. If you "see the Lord" by your own vision, your authority equals or surpasses that of the Twelve and their successors. This seems to entail a form of mysticism in which no distinction is felt between the object seen and the light in which you see it. It follows for the gnostic Valentinus and his group that, as Elaine Pagels explains, "the structure of authority can never be fixed into an institutional framework: it must remain spontaneous, charismatic, and open."[5] In other words, Gnosticism could not be a church: at most, it was a loose affiliation of study groups or mystical cults, open only to initiates. For a member of such a study group, religion was an elaborate experience of one's selfhood, theology was what we call psychology, and the good life was therapeutically animated by knowledge, the experience of insight. Pagels argues that the perspectives and methods of Gnosticism, designed for a few, did not lend themselves to becoming a universal religion:

> In this respect, it was no match for the highly effective system of organization of the catholic church, which expressed a unified religious perspective based on the New Testament canon, offered a creed requiring the initiate to confess only the simplest essentials of faith, and celebrated rituals as simple and profound as baptism and the eucharist.[6]

As an explanation of the victory of the Church over the gnostic heresy, this seems implausible. What early Christians were required to adhere to were not "the simplest essentials of faith." Those essentials included the divine as well as the human nature of Christ, the bodily resurrection, and, before Christian orthodoxy was really established, the Trinity and Transubstantiation. Not simple articles of faith. Christians could assent to these articles without claiming to understand them, but unless you were rotten with cynicism or opportunism, you could not regard them as simple and take them in your stride.

The process of defining Christian orthodoxy began in the second century and was hardly complete by the end of the third. The documents deemed authoritative were the Gospels of Matthew, Mark, Luke, and John, and Paul's Epistle to the Romans. It was a complication that Paul was indifferent to law and office. That the Church was gradually established with a panoply of laws, offices, and hierarchies was largely the work of Tertullian, Origen, Cyprian of Carthage, Eusebius, and Augustine, however diverse those men were. Jerome, Ambrose, and Pope Damasus were effective in giving the Church its Roman and Latin character. But this turn was also the result of changes in the Roman Empire itself by which the Empire came to see the Church not as an enemy but as a mirror image of itself: "it was catholic, universal, ecumenical, orderly, international, multi-racial and increasingly legalistic."[7] The Emperor Constantine's conversion and, in 313, his "Edict of Milan" not only made life easier for Christians but endorsed the clerical and administrative structure of the Church with consequences mixed, at best, for the relation of Church and World.

I am not competent to say what the Church was like or how its energies were disposed in the last week of August 410, when forces under Alaric, although a Christian, entered Rome and pillaged and sacked the city; or two years later when Augustine started writing the *City of God* to defend the Church against the charge that it was responsible for the fall of the Empire. There must have been some in the Church who thought that she should now exert her authority more strenuously than ever. But perhaps there were some who thought that the Church should not assert its authority in worldly terms, lest it fall to forces similar to those that destroyed Rome. Order had to be maintained, but much depended upon whether the Church decided to drive the horse on a tight or a loose rein.

It is my understanding that the Church for a period of several hundred years held to a fairly loose rein with occasional gestures of tightening. I am encouraged in that view by Henry Adams's *Mont-Saint-Michel and Chartres*, but it would not matter greatly if Adams's understanding of the Church in France in the twelfth century turned out to be somewhat fanciful. We are not disputing facts but thinking of two extreme forms of order: the one is insistent, rigorous, and pedantic, the other is such a minimal degree of order as barely consists with its being order at all. Only over a long time could one say which is better.

Adams regarded the thirteenth century as the century of change from a loose to a tight rein:

> Before 1200, the Church seems not to have felt the need of appealing habitually to terror; the promise of hope and happiness was enough; even the portal at Autun, which displays a Last Judgment, belonged to Saint Lazarus the proof and symbol of resurrection. A hundred

years later, every church portal showed Christ not as Saviour but as Judge, and He presided over a Last Judgment at Bourges and Amiens, and here on the south portal, where the despair of the damned is the evident joy of the artist, if it is not even sometimes a little his jest, which is worse. At Chartres Christ is identified with His Mother, the spirit of love and grace, and His Church is the Church Triumphant.[8]

Adams knew that the Church had another face, and that you could see it at Mont-Saint-Michel:

> The Archangel loved heights. Standing on the summit of the tower that crowned his church, wings upspread, sword uplifted, the devil crawling beneath, and the cock, symbol of eternal vigilance, perched on his mailed foot, Saint Michael held a place of his own in heaven and on earth which seems, in the eleventh century, to leave hardly room for the Virgin of the Crypt at Chartres, still less for the Beau Christ of the thirteenth century at Amiens. The Archangel stands for Church and State, and both militant. He is the conqueror of Satan, the mightiest of all created spirits, the nearest to God.[9]

But Adams turns away from Saint Michael as if he embodied the particular face of the medieval Church he did not want to contemplate, the Church of later crusades and the pursuit of Albigensian and other heresies that might well have been let alone. He is in a hurry to come to Chartres.

It is Adams's conviction that the energies of Christian people in the twelfth century were concentrated, in devotion, upon the Virgin, and he offers Chartres in evidence. "The Church at Chartres," he claims, "belonged not to the people, not to the priesthood, and not even to Rome; it belonged to the Virgin."[10] "The Church," he continues, "is wholly given up to the Mother and the Son":

> The Father seldom appears; the Holy Ghost still more rarely. At least, this is the impression made on an ordinary visitor who has no motive to be orthodox; and it must have been the same with the thirteenth-century worshipper who came here with his mind

absorbed in the perfections of Mary. Chartres represents, not the Trinity, but the identity of the Mother and Son. The Son represents the Trinity, which is thus absorbed in the Mother. The idea is not orthodox, but this is no affair of ours. The Church watches over its own.[11]

The artists who did the stone-work and windows at Chartres "were doing their best, not to please a swarm of flat-eared peasants or slow-witted barons, but to satisfy Mary, the Queen of Heaven to whom the Kings and Queens of France were coming constantly for help, and whose absolute power was almost the only restraint recognized by Emperor, pope, and clown."[12] Adams claims that the Virgin was present to the people at Chartres "with a reality that never belonged to her Son or to the Trinity, and hardly to any earthly being, prelate, king, or kaiser. . . . They knew her as well as they knew their own mothers."[13]

If Adams is right, his hymn to the Virgin at Chartres makes it easier for us to understand how ordinary people could accept the official structure of belief without breaking their heads on the difficulty of it. They believed the whole story because of Mary's part in it. They handed over to the Virgin their devotion, and with their devotion their ignorance, their detailed helplessness: they laid their ignorance before her as an offering and trusted her to accept it in that spirit. Adams maintains that their attachment to Mary "rested on an instinct of self-preservation":

> They knew their own peril. If there was to be a future life, Mary was their only hope. She alone represented Love. The Trinity were, or was, One, and could, by the nature of its essence, administer justice alone. Only childlike illusion could expect a personal favour from Christ. Turn the dogma as one would, to this it must logically come. Call the three Godheads by what names one liked, still they must remain One; must administer one justice; must admit only one law. In that law, no human weakness or error could exist; by its essence it was infinite, eternal, immutable. There was no crack and no cranny in the system, through which human frailty could hope to escape. One was forced from corner to corner by a remorseless logic until one fell helpless at Mary's feet.[14]

Adams nearly goes to the extreme point of arguing that Mary put the whole theological structure of Scholasticism at risk and that the risk did not matter to the people and their devotion. All that Mary had to be was fecund. Meditating on the great rose window at Chartres and what it witnesses of human need and feeling, Adams sees no reason to put Mary at the service of law or justice:

> Mary concentrated in herself the whole rebellion of man against fate; the whole protest against divine law; the whole contempt for human law as its outcome; the whole unutterable fury of human nature beating itself against the walls of its prison-house, and suddenly seized by a hope that in the Virgin man had found a door of escape. She was above law; she took feminine pleasure in turning hell into an ornament; she delighted in trampling on every social distinction in this world and the next. She knew that the universe was as unintelligible to her, on any theory of morals, as it was to her worshippers, and she felt, like them, no sure conviction that it was any more intelligible to the Creator of it.[15]

It begins to appear that Mary bends down toward every creature of ignorance and weakness, every man and woman who suffers under law, and that she will not withhold her sympathy from anyone in need of it. Adams says that "the convulsive hold which Mary to this day maintains"—this day being the first years of the twentieth century—"over human imagination—as you can see at Lourdes—was due much less to her power of saving soul or body than to her sympathy with people who suffered under law,—divine or human,—justly or unjustly, by accident or design, by decree of God or by guile of Devil." She cared, he concludes, "not a straw for conventional morality, and she had no notion of letting her friends be punished, to the tenth or any other generation, for the sins of their ancestors or the peccadilloes of Eve."[16] So Adams lets her care for every sorrowing man and woman, as T. S. Eliot does in more subdued tones in the fourth part of "The Dry Salvages," where—thinking of the Church of Notre Dame de la Gard overlooking the sea at Marseilles—he writes:

Lady, whose shrine stands on the promontory,
Pray for all those who are in ships, those
Whose business has to do with fish, and
Those concerned with every lawful traffic
And those who conduct them.

Repeat a prayer also on behalf of
Women who have seen their sons and husbands
Setting forth, and not returning:
Figlia del tuo figlio,
Queen of Heaven.[17]

The phrase from Dante's *Paradiso* and the invocation to the Queen of Heaven bring the prayer back to Rome and Christendom, if not quite to the Virgin of Chartres.

Adams left Chartres at the end of the tenth chapter of his book. He worked on the book at intervals between 1901 and 1904. He published the first version of it in 1905 and a revised version in 1912. But before that he had seen the century run toward a bewildering conclusion with the Chicago Exposition of 1893. The new century started not with a pilgrimage to Chartres but with the great Exposition that opened in Paris on April 15, 1900, and continued with another one, only less impressive, at St. Louis in 1904. Adams had to take account of those, and especially of the fact that "while the force of the Virgin was still felt at Lourdes, and seemed to be as potent as X-rays," in Protestant America "neither Venus nor Virgin ever had value as force—at most as sentiment." No American "had ever been truly afraid of either."[18] So Adams left Chartres to its images and forms, its fear, intercession, and love:

We have done with Chartres. For seven hundred years Chartres has seen pilgrims, coming and going more or less like us, and will perhaps see them for another seven hundred years; but we shall see it no more, and can safely leave the Virgin in her majesty, with her three great prophets on either hand, as calm and confident in their own strength and in God's providence as they were when Saint Louis was born, but looking down from a deserted heaven, into an empty church, on a dead faith.[19]

He did not foresee that in the year 2000 the world would include at least one billion Roman Catholics. Those last coercive phrases of Adams remind us that he had as if from birth the conviction of catastrophe, if not like his friend Henry James the imagination of it: his mind made difficulties for itself, as if that propensity were its only guarantee of being serious. But we have no cause to doubt that he saw the Church in 1900 as having lapsed in every respect and especially in forbearance from the church of 1110 and a century or so thereafter:

> A Church which embraced, with equal sympathy, and within a hundred years, The Virgin, Saint Bernard, William of Champeaux and the School of Saint-Victor, Peter the Venerable, Saint Francis of Assisi, Saint Dominic, Saint Thomas Aquinas, and Saint Bonaventure, was more liberal than any modern State can afford to be. Radical contradictions the State may perhaps tolerate, though hardly, but never embrace or profess. Such elasticity long ago vanished from human thought.[20]

And therefore from other human institutions, not only the Church, Adams implied.

It was probably inevitable that the Catholic Church after the Reformation and the Counter-Reformation thought that its authority must be not only spiritual but practical. In that respect it did not hold itself free from the lessons of modern empire-building and dominion. Indeed, it has been argued that in the later years of the nineteenth century Rome, taking its bearings from modern states, extended its authority over its members far beyond need. It is hard to see what the Church gained, by comparison with what it lost, by the Bull of Papal Infallibility issued in 1870, even though the conditions attached to that infallibility might make it appear almost circumspect. Rome deemed the proclamation of the dogma of the Immaculate Conception to be justified because it defined a devotion of long standing, but the last thing a devotion of long standing needs is definition. The proclamation alienated many of the faithful who felt the devotion but would not take dictation in its favor: they thought there should be only a few dogmas, and that this one was unnecessary. When Cardinal Pecci was elected Pope Leo XIII in 1878, he set about, as he thought, rendering to Caesar the things that were Caesar's and to God the things that were God's. But it was a difficult undertaking, especially in Italy, where the King had just eight years earlier seized the Church's Italian territory and the Pope had to retreat to the Vatican and complain of being ill-used, a complaint eventually stilled by the Lateran Treaty of 1929. But in 1880 Leo XIII thought it necessary to found the Academy of St. Thomas in Rome and to make medieval Scholasticism the official theology of the Church. Biblical scholarship was put under constraint and the Index of prohibited books extended. R. P. Blackmur has commented on these actions:

> The actual triumph of Thomas came in the nineteenth century when he was used to supply the authority in reason which the Church needed to encompass modern science and the combination of popular and dictatorial (non-Christian and anti-clerical) nations into which western society was breaking apart.[21]

But authority is won at a cost—the more authority, the more opportunity for error:

> In one sense the Church was reacting to a materialistic age by excluding the age; but in another and more consequential sense it was following the political states of the age by creating for itself an inclusive authoritarian basis. Where the State gave liberty within its limits and took authority where it could find it, the Church already took the next step and asserted authority without granting liberty, and thus found itself in the common competition for the naked power which it had been its historic and religious mission to redeem by the occult powers of imagination and charity and love.[22]

Leo XIII and later popes regularly intervened in the political machinations of Italy, Germany, and France. In 1895 Leo embarrassed American

Catholic bishops by reflecting on the constitutional separation of Church and State and said that the Church in America "would bring forth more abundant fruits if, in addition to liberty, she enjoyed the favour of the laws and the patronage of public authority."[23] The bishops had learnt to live with the separation of Church and State; they did not appreciate having a feasible balance of interests disturbed.

But many factors worked to thwart Rome's authoritarian zeal. First of these was the increasing discrepancy between one's private and one's public life. Simmel's book *The Philosophy of Money* is still our best guide to this feeling. He argues that the modern division of labor "permits the number of dependencies to increase just as it causes personalities to disappear behind their functions, because only one side of them operates, at the expense of all those others the composition of which would make up a personality." "On the one hand," Simmel maintains, "money makes possible the plurality of economic dependencies through its infinite flexibility and divisibility, while on the other it is conducive to the removal of the personal element from human relationships through its indifferent and objective nature."[24] As a result, people in the later years of the nineteenth century tended to conduct their public and professional lives in accordance with the prevailing financial and materialist values, but at the same time they regarded this part of their lives as specious. They felt that their true lives were lived within as a personal form of Romanticism. Individuals pursued their development as an inner drama rather than as a willing engagement with the contents of the objective culture. Besides, as Adams remarks in *Mont-Saint-Michel and Chartres*, we have to allow for that "nineteenth-century indifference which refuses to be interested in what it cannot understand,"[25] a matter of moment for members of a Church founded to preserve a story requiring faith, and mysteries beyond elucidation. Simmel doesn't mention another form of the division of labor, the habit—which Max Weber elucidated—by which people concede the right of judgment in large areas of their external lives to experts—politicians, bankers, economists—and retain as sacrosanct their private relation to themselves. Especially in America, where the combined force of individualism and Protestantism is so strong, it is almost inevitable that for many people, including Roman Catholics, religion becomes a matter of conscience, a value hard to distinguish from one's desires. It is evident that many people remain in the Church while deciding for themselves when they have sinned and when not: they remain in the Church by insisting on the ultimate authority of their consciences and ignoring the Church's instruction on divorce, remarriage, and artificial means of contraception. Some are prepared to make a case for abortion, assisted suicide, and euthanasia. Many do not fulfill their Easter duty of going to confession before receiving the Eucharist. The concept of an informed conscience is the traditional discipline to be imposed upon one's desires in such matters, and the Church is supposed to provide instruction in that respect, but it is easy to blur the distinction between these values and to settle for the messages your heart delivers.

Still, the Church is in the world and must remain there. But how? I want to consider two quite different visions of the Church and its presence in the world. I have taken the title of this lecture from Hans Urs von Balthasar's *Church and World*, and I would recite more of the substance of the book if I could emulate his high rhapsodic style. Perhaps I can give something of his theology at whatever cost to the plenitude of its detail. If nothing else, the contrast between Balthasar and Adams ought to show the latitude of interpretation possible when the theme is the different ways in which the Church has been active in the world.

Balthasar begins with a distinction between the Old Covenant and the New. In the Old Testament, he maintains, the crucial relation was between God and the people. The great figures—Moses, Abraham, David, Job, Judith, Esther—are in the end personifications of the people and the people's destiny. In the Old Testament, sin and redemption always have a collective rather than an individual bearing. But in the New Testament the individual stands alone as a person before God. The central act of conversion is this rising into the awareness of one's reality, which is called into being by the encounter with Christ:

> All of this is eminently personal. It is always the individual, the person, who stands before Jesus. Even when he addresses a crowd, he speaks to the individual. The Sermon on the Mount is a good example of this, where the address varies from "You" (in the plural) to "you" in the singular in a rapid and bewildering manner. This "you" is already ecclesial, wherein each individual recognizes himself as the

"you" who is meant and who is personally commanded. This is why in the Church no "I" can hide behind a "we" when deep commitment is made to God and Christ. Every person is considered individually.[26]

In the same spirit Balthasar makes much of the episode in Mark in which Jesus cures the blind man at Bethsaida. The man is brought to him by others, but Jesus takes him by the hand and leads him out of the town:

> . . . and when he had spit on his eyes, and put his hands upon him, he asked him if he saw ought. And he looked up, and said, I see men as trees, walking. After that he put his hands again upon his eyes, and made him look up: and he was restored, and saw every man clearly. And he sent him away to his house, saying, Neither go into the town, nor tell it to any in the town. (8:22–26)

Balthasar says of this episode:

> Here the singling out is done by distancing the place, but while this is done the man is led by the hand. It is a walk into solitude, led by Jesus.[27]

Balthasar has been rebuked for this emphasis. It is acknowledged that he takes seriously time, history, and the world, but there have been complaints that the effect of his distinction between the Old Covenant and the New is that, as in the *Spiritual Exercises* of St. Ignatius, "it is the history of the individual subject that interests him."[28] Balthasar emphasizes that "the Church is uniquely the sphere which binds God and creature together,"[29] but the Church, even as a community, is for him a place of solitude: the individual is alone there.[30] No defect in the institution is entailed, but the communal aspect of the Church is a later and perhaps secondary consideration.

Balthasar retains the "personalism" of his theology by presenting the Church by way of an analogy with Christ:

> 'As the Father has sent me, so I send you.' In this line is expressed the continuation of Christ's descending movement. As Christ fulfills the

will of the Father precisely by going away from the Father and so remains one with the Father, so too the Church fulfills the will of Christ in her going into the world and so remains one with him.[31]

The Church, by being sent into the world, is fundamentally a part of the world, just as Christ as man was a part of the world. The naturalness of the Church is visible in all her functions—the sacraments, liturgy, theology, and ethics. This does not mean that Church and World are one and the same, but that the Church, as Balthasar says, "walks in the path of redemption by plunging into the world and becoming herself the tool of this redemption, the *instrumentum redemptionis*."[32] Balthasar emphasizes "the crucial importance of humanity and worldliness as the place of the epiphany of the ever-greater and ever-more-inconceivable God."[33] But he seems to have no role for the Church in the world other than to facilitate the salvation of souls.

Balthasar sees Mary both in relation to the individual and to the Church. For the individual, she is the very type of contemplation:

> She is the model which should govern contemplation, if it is to keep clear of two dangers: one, that of seeing the Word only as something external, instead of the profoundest mystery within our own being, that in which we live and move and are; the other, that of regarding the Word as so interior to us that we confuse it with our own being, with a natural wisdom given us once and for all, and ours to use as we will.[34]

Mary, in Balthasar's tribute, reminds us of the Lady in the second part of Eliot's "Ash-Wednesday," where the litany resumes alien experiences reconciled in her:

> Lady of silences
> Calm and distressed
> Torn and most whole
> Rose of memory
> Rose of forgetfulness
> Exhausted and life-giving
> Worried reposeful.[35]

Mary's relation to the Church, according to Balthasar, is that she is the supreme exemplar of spirituality, prior to all differentiations into more specific forms of spirituality.[36] In none of her capacities does she resemble the object of popular piety ascribed by Adams to the Virgin of Chartres.

The second version of the Church and its presence in the world I want to consider is John Milbank's. I understand that he is part of a Roman Catholic movement in England called Radical Orthodoxy. His book *Theology and Social Theory* (1990) is subtitled *Beyond Secular Theory*. The book is extraordinarily far-ranging, but I will look mainly at its last chapters, where Milbank offers to say how the Church should conduct itself in the world. He starts with an attack on Aquinas for, in effect, inventing the separation of Church and State:

> It is true that Aquinas, like Augustine, does not recognize any real justice that is not informed by charity, and that he has, in consequence, moved not very far down the road which allows a sphere of secular autonomy; nevertheless he has moved, and he has moved too far. By beginning to see social, economic and administrative life as essentially natural, and part of a political sphere separate from the Church, Aquinas opens the way to regarding the Church as an organization specializing in what goes on inside men's souls.[37]

Milbank's point is that once "the political is seen as a permanent natural sphere, pursuing positive finite ends, then, inevitably, firm lines of division arise between what is "secular" and what is "spiritual." Moreover,

> a Church more narrowly defined as a cure of souls is also a Church granting more power to the regular clergy over both monastics and laity. And a Church which understands itself as having a particular sphere of interest will mimic the procedures of political sovereignty, and invent a kind of bureaucratic management of believers.[38]

Milbank wants to keep the bounds between Church and State very hazy. He wants to see the "social" existence of many complex and interlocking powers emerge to forestall either a sovereign State or a hierarchical Church. The action of the Church in the world should be clearest in parishes, small groups sharing common goals. The Church should be a haven, a place for the forgiveness of sin, an institution that has replaced all tragic profundity by conviviality.

I have no objection to the conviviality, but I object to the implication in Milbank's book that religion should be replaced by politics, a new interruptive politics, to be sure. Objecting to the separation of Church and State, he wants the Church to assume the functions of a perfect State and theology to become a counter-politics. He seems not much concerned with Balthasar's first care, the saving of an individual soul within a Church mindful of existential loneliness. Milbank's book ends with a stark offer to the Church:

> In the midst of history, the judgment of God has already happened. And either the Church enacts the vision of paradisal community which this judgment opens out, or else it promotes a hellish society beyond any terrors known to antiquity: *corruptio optimi pessima*. For the Christian interruption of history 'decoded' antique virtue, yet thereby helped to unleash first liberalism and then nihilism. Insofar as the Church has failed, and has even become a hellish anti-Church, it has confined Christianity, like everything else, within the cycle of the ceaseless exhaustion and return of violence.
>
> Yet as we are situated on the far side of the cross—the event of the judgment of God—no return to law, to the antique compromise of inhibition of violence, remains possible. Both nihilism and Christianity decode the inconsistencies of this position. And the absolute Christian vision of ontological peace now provides the only alternative to a nihilistic outlook. Even today, in the midst of the self-torturing circle of secular reason, there can open to view again a series with which it is in no continuity: the emanation of harmonious difference, the exodus of new generations, the path of peaceful flight. . . .[39]

I'm not sure that Milbank's vision requires a Church at all: there would be no need of such an institution if his politics or counter-politics were to succeed in transforming the world. But it is fanciful—far more fanciful than any vision in Henry Adams's phrases—to think that distinctions maintained for seven hundred years between secular and spiritual realms, as between Church and State or Church and World, are likely to be set aside. The world is so assured of its success that it is most unlikely to resort to a sublime theology for its further enlightenment. We are left with a world that succeeds by its own lights and fails tragically when it fails at all—its failures are starvation, poverty, violence, hatred, murder. Balthasar's vision needs a Church to extend and embody the analogy of Father and Son, and to shelter the soul in its loneliness. But Balthasar pays small tribute to Caesar or to social experience in general. Where Milbank would turn the Church into a redeemed world according to a counter-politics of his own making, Balthasar would turn the world into a redeemed Church for the most part silent, knees bent in prayer and contemplation.

These considerations lead at once to the question: since the Church is indeed in the world, how should it comport itself there? It would be agreeable to speak of the Church not as it is in practice but as it should or might be, according to the idea of its mission, but it would be futile to avoid the question of its practices altogether. I will beg off saying much about Vatican II in relation to authority and the loss of it, mainly because my sense of the Council is still insecure. I am aware that many members of the Church felt in 1962 and perhaps still feel that the summoning of the Council opened the Church to a new day of speech, responsiveness, and listening. I have not been one of those. Millions of words later, I still can't estimate what the Church has gained and lost by Pope John XXIII's initiative. I note that Balthasar is rather gruff about some of its consequences. "The Church since the Council," he says, "has to a large extent put off its mystical characteristics; it has become a Church of permanent conversations, organizations, advisory commissions, congresses, synods, commissions, academies, parties, pressure groups, functions, structures and restructurings, sociological experiments, statistics."[40] I, too, miss the silence. I am also nostalgic for the Latin Mass and Gregorian Chant, but those losses, I accept, are small by comparison with the accessibility of the Mass to the faithful through the vernacular languages. But there have been blunders. It seems to me to have been a grave error of judgment for Paul VI to reserve to himself the adjudication of two issues— contraception and clerical celibacy. The publication of *Humanae Vitae* in

1968 did not undo the damage. I acknowledge that the Church before and after Vatican II has developed a noble social teaching, as expressed in encyclicals by Leo XIII, Paul VI, and John Paul II. Paul's *Nostra Aetate* (1965) removed the collective burden of guilt from the Jewish people, however belatedly, and condemned "all hatreds, persecutions, displays of anti-Semitism levelled at any time or from any source against the Jews."[41] John Paul has maintained this condemnation and extended it on several occasions. Paul's *Populorum Progressio* (1967) attacked the structural injustices endemic in capitalism, and called for particular care for those in need of it—refugees, migrants, victims. In *Salvifici Doloris* (1984) John Paul offered a remarkably positive commentary on human suffering in relation to the sufferings of Christ. In *Sollicitudo Rei Socialis* (1987) he made the analysis of *Populorum Progressio* even more pointed, referring to "structures of sin" and the evil of succumbing to market forces. John Paul's *Tertio Millenio Adveniente* (1994) calls for the alleviation of Third World indebtedness. His *Evangelium Vitae* (1995) is a diagnosis of the "culture of death," a crucial document in relation to abortion and euthanasia. These and other interventions denote one of the Church's crucial ways of acting responsibly in the world.

But I note, too, that many things done by the same Popes have been at best wayward and at worst insensitive. John Paul II has been accused of being "at odds with his own thoughts."[42] I think this is true, especially of his actions in the past few years of his illness and pain. I don't understand why he chose an ostensibly ecumenical occasion to assert the provenance of indulgences, or why he has canonized 280 new saints, and moved—in *Ex corde ecclesiae* (1990)—toward an unnecessarily specific and controlling relation between Rome and Catholic universities in the United States. There are far more urgent matters than that to be attended to. Perhaps the most urgent is that the Church must restore the founding mysteries, without appearing to domesticate them or explain them away. It must tell the story over and over again. It must not take the easy way out, reducing theology to popular psychology, evading the dark parts of the Old Testament and the New.

If it does these hard things, the Church will find itself at odds with the world. So it should. The Church should expect to have a mainly antagonistic relation to the world, and be ready to denounce its specific crimes: the conduct of war by indiscriminate bombing and the killing of civilians, the retention of the death penalty, genetic experimentation, the structural crimes committed in the cause of profit. Indeed, the separation of Church and State, as in the United States, has at least this advantage, that it enables the Church at once to be in the world and to stand aside from its purposes. I agree with the late John Howard Yoder that the Church should not engage in what he called "Constantinianism," the assumption of responsibility for the moral structure of non-Christian society.[43] I agree, too, with Stanley Hauerwas and William Willimon when they call upon Christians to live as "resident aliens" in modern America.[44] Resident aliens pay their taxes, but they do not vote in state or general elections: they live in society at a distance from its ideology. I note, too, that the experience of having Church and State ostensibly at one, in my own country, has proved a specious blessing. In Ireland, the constitution of 1937 recognized the "special position" of the Catholic Church. It took the Church fifty years to realize that it gained nothing by this special relation and that the occasions on which it exercised its influence on matters that most people would regard as political and governmental turned out badly. In recent years the Church has been quite content to see the reference to its special character in Ireland removed from the constitution. There appears to be no alternative to the American constitutional arrangement that keeps Church and State officially and for most purposes separate. The Church is then in a better position to be vigilant and to criticize the State and the World where such criticism is warranted. And while speaking out on these issues, the Church must confess its historical sins, as the Pope has recently confessed them, its acts of cruelty and persecution.

The philosopher John Anderson has maintained, with Heraclitus as his authority, that we ought to ask of any social institution not what end or purpose it serves but what conflicts it is the scene.[45] The main conflict of which the Church is the scene is between "Render to Caesar the things that are Caesar's and to God the things that are God's" and a claim equally momentous: "My Kingdom is not of this world."

FOUR

OTHERWISE THAN BEING

MY THEME IS THE ETHICAL TURN IN CRITICISM AND PHILOSOPHY. Twenty or thirty years ago there was a linguistic turn in literary criticism, and a few years later a political turn. These preoccupations have not become archaic or redundant, but I observe that some of the most formidable scholars are now arguing that reading as such is an ethical act, and perhaps the representative one. This turn could be documented over a longer period by referring to Iris Murdoch, Charles Taylor, Bernard Williams, Alasdair MacIntyre, Paul Ricoeur, J. Hillis Miller, Jacques Derrida, and other scholars. But I think there may be an advantage in concentrating on the ethics of Emmanuel Levinas before looking at a work of fiction. Levinas reached the ethical emphasis of *Totality and Infinity* and *Otherwise than Being, or, Beyond Essence* only after many years of more orthodox philosophic writing. I'll assume agreement that ethics and morality are not the same. I take ethics to be a system of reflection on one's actions, and morality the application of the conclusions derived from ethics—it is ethics in practice. I am aware that Bernard Williams and other philosophers make a different distinction and treat morality as a special (and problematic) form of ethical theory.

In his early professional years Levinas was mainly concerned with the introduction of Husserl's version of phenomenology to French intellectual life. "For a whole generation of students and readers of *Logical Investigations*," he recalls, "phenomenology, heralding a new atmosphere in European philosophy, meant mainly thought's access to being."[1] More specifically:

'The return to the things themselves,' the rallying cry of phenom-
enology, is most often understood as that priority of being over the
consciousness in which it shows itself, dictating its Law to the acts of
consciousness and their synthesis.[2]

Husserl insisted upon "the intentional character of consciousness"[3] and
regarded as naive the thought that is absorbed by objects. Levinas agreed.
He admired Husserl for repudiating dogmatic metaphysics, submitting
the concept of Being to phenomenal appearances, paying proper atten-
tion to intuition, questioning the traditional account of thinking as con-
templating, and emphasizing the intentional or transitive character of
understanding. Levinas argued that one's consciousness should act upon
a better intention than the puny one of gaining access to being: it should
take up "the wonder of a mode of thought better than knowledge."[4] In the
end, Levinas decided that Husserl was still immured in the assumption
that all thought is knowledge, and that knowledge is founded on the inter-
pretation of being as living presence. Great philosopher as he was, Husserl
had not done enough to curb the possessive zeal of knowing, the determi-
nation of the mind to absorb into its interiority any and every object of
attention. A reader of Husserl was free to enforce the grasping self.

Heidegger was a more formidable master than Husserl. When Le-
vinas first read *Sein und Zeit*, he did not see in it any indication of "a
political or violent ulterior motive,"[5] but he was not sure. Early on, "per-
haps even before 1933 and certainly after Hitler's huge success at the time
of his election to the Reichstag," Levinas had been told by Alexandre Koyré
that Heidegger was in sympathy with National Socialism. Levinas was
dismayed but hoped that Heidegger's sentiment expressed "only the tem-
porary lapse of a great speculative mind into practical banality."[6] But it
was a frail hope. Levinas gradually came to think that Heidegger's entire
philosophy might be corrupt. He began to ask himself how *Sein und Zeit*
could so easily do without an ethical sense; why in Heidegger's philoso-
phy the relation to a particular person is so blithely displaced by an
abstraction, that of Being. Levinas wondered why Heidegger insisted on
the priority of universal, anonymous Being over the existence of you and
me; and why he thought it important to say that "we have our residence

in the distinction between beings and being."[7] As Levinas said in *Totality and Infinity:*

> The primacy of ontology for Heidegger does not rest on the truism: "to know the *existent*, it is necessary to have comprehended the Being of the existent." To affirm the priority of *Being* over the *existent* is already to decide the essence of philosophy; it is to subordinate the relation with *someone*, who is an existent, (the ethical relation), to a relation with the *Being of the existent*, which, impersonal, permits the apprehension, the domination of the existent (a relationship of knowing), subordinates justice to freedom.[8]

It is certainly not from Heidegger, as Levinas says in an unusually severe mood, "that one should take lessons on the love of man or social justice."[9] Heidegger's philosophy eventually seemed to Levinas ethically indifferent, a nasty cult of the neuter rather than of masculine or feminine; a philosophy raging for the totality in which individuals are mere particles or instances. "*Dasein* in Heidegger is never hungry," Levinas maintained.[10]

By 1947, with the publication of *De l'existence à l'existant*, Levinas had turned against Western philosophy so far as it was preoccupied with questions of being and knowledge. In *Totality and Infinity* and *Otherwise than Being* he develops his disagreements with Husserl and Heidegger into an attack on the entire philosophic enterprise of the West. He finds it repellent that this philosophy has been fixated on ontology and epistemology:

> The relation with Being that is enacted as ontology consists in neutralizing the existent in order to comprehend or grasp it. It is hence not a relation to the other as such but the reduction of the other to the same. . . . For possession affirms the other, but within a negation of its independence. "I think" comes down to "I can,"—to an appropriation of what is, to an exploitation of reality. Ontology as first philosophy is a philosophy of power. . . . Possession is preeminently the form in which the other becomes the same, by becoming mine.[11]

According to Levinas, political totalitarianism is a consequence of ontology. It follows that "one has to find for man another kinship than that which ties him to being."[12] Epistemology is also guilty, because "through knowledge, whether one wants it or not, the object is absorbed by the subject and duality disappears."[13] Levinas deplores the fact that "philosophy is the bearer of the spirituality of the West, where spirit is taken to be coextensive with knowing."[14]

He deplores, therefore, any system of thought that claims total competence:

> The visage of being that shows itself in war is fixed in the concept of totality, which dominates Western philosophy. Individuals are reduced to being bearers of forces that command them unbeknown to themselves. The meaning of individuals (invisible outside of this totality) is derived from the totality.[15]

In *Ethics and Infinity* Levinas attacks the philosophy of the West as "an attempt at universal synthesis, a reduction of all experience, of all that is reasonable, to a totality wherein consciousness embraces the world, leaves nothing other outside of itself, and thus becomes absolute thought."[16] For the same reason he denounces the motives at work in Idealism, myth, and mysticism: each of these he regards as totalitarian. The only philosophers who escape Levinas's censure are Plato, in his concern for the Good, and Descartes, in his recognition of the infinite that exceeds one's grasp.

Levinas's own position is that "first philosophy is an ethics."[17] Ethics precedes ontology.[18] I take this to mean: take care of ethics and let ontology and epistemology look out for themselves. If we were to allow ethics to precede ontology, we would so live that questions of being, knowledge, the self, and power would become secondary considerations. Every act of the mind would be subject to criteria not of truth but of justice. The primary consideration would be the quality of my relation to other people, my responsibility for each of them. Levinas has often quoted, as an example of that emphasis, the passage in *The Brothers Karamazov* in which Alyosha says: "We are all responsible for everyone else, but I am more responsible than all the others." To this he has added a statement of Rabbi Israel

Salanter: "the material needs of my neighbor are my spiritual needs."[19] Psalm 119, too, is close to Levinas's mind: "I am a stranger on earth, hide not thy commandments from me." The condition of being strangers and slaves in Egypt, Levinas says, "brings man close to his neighbor. . . . No one is at home. The memory of this servitude assembles humanity."[20]

Levinas's ethics does not rest on a concept or an argument, it is an attitude, spontaneous and primordial, leading to an action, a response that does not wait for reasons. Above all, it does not wait for a concept of duty. If it seeks reasons or concepts, it is then on the way to becoming something else and less—theory, law, or politics. In this respect Levinas differs from Derrida, who maintains that to lack a 'thematization' of responsibility is to be irresponsible, even though an adequate thematization is impossible:

> We must continually remind ourselves that some part of irresponsibility insinuates itself wherever one demands responsibility without sufficiently conceptualizing and thematizing what 'responsibility' means; that is to say everywhere. One can say everywhere a priori and nonempirically, for if the complex linkage between the theoretical and practical . . . is, quite clearly, irreducible, then the heterogeneity between the two linked orders is just as irreducible. Hence, the activating of responsibility (decision, act, praxis) will always take place before and beyond any theoretical or thematic determination. It will have to decide without it, independently from knowledge; that will be the condition of a practical idea of freedom.[21]

Such a quandary doesn't trouble Levinas. In his ethics, the primary act is the spontaneous one by which I address another person as "you." I ground my own mode of existence solely upon that act. No theory or concept is required: my solicitude should not wait for a theorem, it is as originary as discourse. "The essence of discourse is ethical."[22] All recourse to words, Levinas maintains, "takes place already within the primordial face-to-face of language."[23] Especially of language in the vocative rather than the nominative case. Prior to my acknowledgment of another person, I am at best a grammatical or ontological subject. By the gratuitous act of acknowledging another person, I too become a person. Every such act is particular: "the collectivity in which I say 'you' or 'we' is not a plural of the 'I'."[24] The auspices under which I say "you" are ethical and social but not exclusive: the aim is not to have a love affair but to animate a community. Not that Levinas, at least in his early work, denies me my inner life. The social relation is "preeminently experience"[25] but "the inner life is the unique *way* for the real to exist as a plurality."[26] In later work, he became much more suspicious of the inner life, repudiated its mystery, and thought it justified only when it was mainly engaged in populating its space, adding other people to its cognition.

Levinas's parable for the ethics he recommends is Abraham's unquestioning response to God in Genesis 22. Before he knows what God wants or that he is to go to Moriah, or for what purpose, Abraham says "hineni," meaning simply "Here I am." In "The Trace of the Other" Levinas makes a sharp contrast between Abraham and Homer's Odysseus in this respect:

> The God of the philosophers from Aristotle to Leibniz by way of the god of the scholastics is a god adequate to reason, a comprehended god who could not trouble the autonomy of consciousness, which finds itself again in all its adventures, returning home to itself like Odysseus, who through all his peregrinations is only on the way to his native land. . . . To the myth of Odysseus returning to Ithaca, we would like to oppose the story of Abraham leaving his homeland forever for a land yet unknown.[27]

Abraham's unquestioning "Here I am" stands for other instances of gratuitousness, notably for the act by which Israelites accepted the Torah before coming to know its import. Explicating Rabbi Eleazar's reference to the Israelites "doing before hearing," Levinas says that the doing which is at stake here "is not simply *praxis* as opposed to theory but a way of *actualizing without beginning with the possible*."[28]

Levinas's philosophy is not, however, foundational; it doesn't appeal to a concept of human nature from which certain attitudes, values, and deeds supposedly ensue. Nor does he attempt the impossible task of moving from the true to the good, from description to prescription, from the indicative to the imperative mood. For him, ethical life starts with a prescription, a command as if from God, eliciting a response, a spontaneous act, that of my saying "you." But by asserting that such-and-such an act is "primordial," Levinas comes within an ace of appealing to a theory of human nature. I don't see how he differs, in this respect, from Matthew Arnold in *Culture and Anarchy*. Arnold doesn't explicitly base his persuasions on a theory of human nature or natural law, but he urges me to rise to my "best self." He has no evidence for the existence of such a capacity in me, except that the self I ordinarily act upon can hardly be my best one. When Levinas says that ethics precedes ontology, he evidently means: live as if ethics had the authority of a primordial motive, such that without it there would be no life in you at all; live by that axiom, even though I can't claim that it is natural or self-evident for you to do so.

This seems to make his philosophy akin to Buber's in *I and Thou*. In *Outside the Subject* Levinas praises Buber's I-Thou relation as the "primal word," ultimately "the opening condition of all language, even the language that states the relation of pure knowledge expressed by the *Grundwort Ich-Es* (I-That)."[29] But Levinas criticizes Buber for making the relation between I and Thou reciprocal. I will acknowledge you, then you will acknowledge me: fifty-fifty. From this reciprocity a community begins to form. But that is not enough for Levinas. Nor is it enough to say, as Michel de Certeau does, that the self is not singular but plural and social. Levinas is willing to concede that "equality between persons" is a good enough basis for "the political order of citizens in a state."[30] But it is not radical enough for ethics. According to *Totality and Infinity* and *Otherwise than Being*, I should acknowledge you as the irreducible person you are whether you acknowledge me or not. As in love, one resigns oneself to not being loved : "Dans l'amour—à moins de ne pas aimer d'amour—il faut se résigner à ne pas être aimé."[31] It is only by acknowledging you that I come to be myself. Until I make that commitment, I can merely insist upon being my sole self, as in the sordid rhetoric of individualism. When I acknowledge you, a society begins to form: it is a community of people who feel themselves addressed. They hold themselves responsible: they enjoy their freedom only after hearing themselves addressed and after responding. A society is a gathering together of those who speak and listen. With this emphasis, Levinas restores the quality that seemed to have receded from his sense of life: enjoyment, conviviality, the pleasure of face-to-face.

There is another difference between Levinas and Buber. The appearing of you to me, by Levinas's standards, is not a cognitive event. In Buber it is, or so Levinas thinks. So in *Outside the Subject* Levinas rebukes Buber for allowing the philosophy of dialogue to remain "within the *element* of consciousness" and subject to "a thought that knows." Further:

> Does Buber's language, so faithful to the novelty of the relation with others in contrast with the knowledge going toward being, break entirely with the priority of ontology? Is not I-Thou spoken as its own way of reaching being?[32]

Levinas thinks it deplorable that the rhetorical verve of *I and Thou* should aid such a horrible cause. Similarly with Gabriel Marcel. Buber and Marcel say: In the beginning was neither the Word nor the deed but the relation. But Marcel, like Buber, remains "deeply rooted, despite all the disruption introduced by the idea of Thou, in ontology."[33] For that reason, Levinas is much closer to Franz Rosenzweig than to Buber or Marcel. In *The Star of Redemption* Rosenzweig attacked ontology for much the same reason as Levinas did: it asks the wrong question, "what is . . .?", and gives morally damaging answers.

Levinas's problem is: How to change philosophy from within and despite having to use its words? How to escape from the self-serving prejudice inscribed in ontology and epistemology? Levinas's answer starts personally: by being a Jew. In that role he epitomizes the Ten Commandments as one: Thou Shalt Not Kill. "My work," he says, "is situated in the fullness of the documents, beliefs and moral practices that characterize the positive fact of Judaism."[34] It follows that Levinas's aim is to displace the priority of knowledge by the priority of faith: not faith in God but in the sublime existence of other people than oneself. Not faith in their mere bodily proximity on the street, but in their mode of existence as persons for whom I hold myself responsible. What Levinas believes is clear enough. God comes into the story because He is in the Bible, but He rarely comes into Levinas's reckoning. Levinas's God has had the wisdom, apparently, to abdicate in favor of His children: "It is a great glory for God to have created a being capable of seeking Him or of hearing Him from afar, having experienced separation, having experienced atheism."[35] Henceforth, no relation to God can be direct or immediate:

> The Divine can be manifested only through my neighbour. For a Jew, Incarnation is neither possible nor necessary. After all, the formula for this comes from Jeremiah 22:16: 'He judged the course of the poor and needy: then it was well. Is not this to know me, says the Lord.'[36]

But God, before abdicating, put the Torah into the hands of His children. As the Talmud says: "So should it be that you would forsake me, but would keep my Torah." Not surprisingly, Levinas thinks himself justified in "loving the Torah more than God," if only because God is not sufficiently there to be loved. Levinas often seems to love the Torah instead of loving God, and grounds this choice on the claim that it is better to love the Torah than to cultivate the madness of seeking direct contact with God unmediated by reason. Christianity has its own way of dealing with this. Direct contact with God is impossible and should not be sought. The gap between human beings and God is absolute. The incarnate Christ is at once divine and human, and therefore a sufficient mediator. Enough is enough. Levinas is hostile to Christianity in this respect, as he is bound to be, given his indifference to the Incarnation and the historical person of Christ. Rather than speak of God as Creator, Levinas has recourse to "the third person, to what I have called *illeity*, to speak of the Infinite and the divine transcendence, which is other than the alterity of others."[37] The difference claimed in that last clause is not clear to me. In Levinas's books, religion soon yields to philosophy—in a transfigured sense— which in quick measure becomes ethics and thereafter politics. Otherwise put: Levinas's religion is primarily an ethical experience, construed by reason Hebraic rather than Greek. Hebraic reason is what we would all practice if the philosophy of the West had taken a different course, talmudic rather than scholastic, ethical rather than epistemological. In the end, Levinas's God is all the other people.

Derrida is correct, therefore, to say that Levinas can't distinguish between the alterity of God and that of any person:

Kierkegaard would have to admit, as Levinas reminds him, that ethics is also the order of and respect for absolute singularity, and not only that of the generality or of the repetition of the same. He cannot therefore distinguish so conveniently between the ethical and the religious. But for his part, in taking into account absolute singularity, that is, the absolute alterity obtaining in relations between one human and another, Levinas is no longer able to distinguish between the infinite alterity of God and that of every human. His ethics is already a religious one.[38]

Again, I don't think the distinction between ethics and religion, and the difficulty of maintaining it, troubles Levinas: he is always willing to see religion taking the form of ethics.

Levinas is a philosopher, not a theologian, and he must do the best he can with concepts he regards as morally defective. This explains why the work he has set himself, to translate Hebrew into Greek, means "to articulate in Greek the principles that Greece ignored."[39] It is not easy. Derrida has pondered, in his first essay on Levinas, "the necessity of lodging oneself within traditional conceptuality in order to destroy it," and he has argued that Levinas's metaphysics presupposes the phenomenology it seeks to question.[40] Levinas knows this well enough, and replies that Derrida is in the same predicament. But Levinas doesn't regard the problem as lethal. He has insisted, at least once and perhaps with politics rather than ontology in mind, that "we must have recourse to the medium of full understanding and comprehension, in which all truth is reflected—that is, to the Greek civilization and what it engendered: *logos*, the coherent discourse of reason, life in a reasonable State."[41]

Is Levinas's position in philosophy at all persuasive? In *La Sagesse de l'amour* (1984) Alain Finkielkraut brought Levinas's philosophy to bear upon readings of Flaubert, Henry James, Proust, Roland Barthes, Condorcet, Tocqueville, and other writers, but he also raised a question: isn't Levinas's philosophy predicated upon people as we should be rather than as we are? From Hobbes to Adam Smith, one tradition of philosophy has acted on the understanding that people are not moral beings, that ethics is not natural. Finkielkraut answers his question by saying that nonetheless Levinas is not a philosopher of altruism; he does not indulge himself in vaguely hopeful sentiments, pity, or pathos. But Finkielkraut gives some of the show away by saying that ethics, in Levinas, is an act of transformation. I am to put my nature in question, face-to-face with another person: "Ethics is my nature called into question by the face of the Other."[42] But suppose I don't want to put my nature in question, or to bother noticing the Other? Levinas is urging me to replace one form of spontaneity, my egoism—to be or not to be, as the sole question—with a better one, according to which my obligation to the Other is not a decision I make but an expression of his or her call. I may not want this expression, but I must have it or cease being human.

There is a more fundamental problem. Like Kant in the *Critique of Practical Reason*, Levinas can't deduce ethical laws from experience and therefore must posit them. In "The Rights of Man and the Rights of the Other" he can say only that these rights "are based on an original sense of the right, or the sense of an original right."[43] Whose sense? Mine? And if mine, how did I get it? Levinas refers to "the patency of the rights of man,"[44] but he can't explain how they are patent or to whom. The words "patent" and "original" have to do immense work here, and even after the work we have to take them on trust. It is like saying "Let ABC be a triangle," an agreement we make because of the gratifications that ensue. Another problem: has Levinas succeeded in prescribing his ethics anywhere but in being? He has hardly surpassed the philosophy of essence, being, and knowledge merely by saying, with due iteration, *beyond essence*. I can't see that he has succeeded where Buber and Marcel have failed, in establishing an "otherwise than being." I think he has disturbed the complacency of the West—or would disturb it if his work were fully acknowledged. He has set many doubts astir among the ostensible certitudes of ontology and epistemology. But he has not disabled these projects. It is still feasible to posit an ethics within the axioms of Being.

Levinas seems to me remarkably unworldly: much as he hates abstraction, he often seems to be merely moving abstractions around on the page. He rarely goes back to the rough ground of detail. I appreciate that he is dealing with ethical principles, and that morality and politics in his view come later. But it is perturbing that he rarely acknowledges the minute particulars of anyone's life; even of his own, which I assume was rich in detail, much of it appalling. But we would never know of his tragedies if we had to wait for him to speak of them. Even in his political writings he has a remarkable inclination to keep a zone of silence at the center of the discourse. Sometimes his strategy seems disingenuous. In *Difficult Freedom* he writes several essays on Judaism and modern Israel but not a word about Israel's Other, the Palestinians. He often gives the impression that only Jews have suffered. I find it odd that an ethics so high-principled rarely considers what is happening in the streets.

It might be possible to write Levinas off as an artist, a poet, a prophet or visionary who had only one thing to say: Ethics precedes Ontology. As a general reader, I admire him for the resourcefulness he showed in attempting an adversary form of thinking. "Is this not the problem of philosophy," he asks, "affording a glimpse of itself before the appearance of things, substances and general ideas?"[45] A glimpse is the most he has shown, but it is something. It is edifying, too, that he denounced "the solipsistic anxiety of consciousness seeing itself in all its adventures as captivated by itself."[46] That needed to be said, after centuries of angst, often self-induced. Levinas was not of course alone in attacking the tradition of philosophy from Parmenides to Heidegger, in which the leading words are consciousness, self, identity, being, subject, and object. Habermas said as much in *The Philosophic Discourse of Modernity* (1985): "The paradigm of the philosophy of consciousness is exhausted."[47] Richard Rorty, too, has been saying that "unfortunately, many philosophers, especially in the English-speaking world, are still trying to hold on to the Platonic insistence that the principal duty of human beings is to *know*."[48] But Habermas and Rorty want to see philosophy becoming politics. Levinas wanted to see it starting and persisting as ethics. I assume that ethics precedes politics.

I I

It is not surprising, in view of Levinas's commitment to Greek philosophy—even in the act of making it acknowledge the ethical force of Hebrew—that he is hostile to art, literature, and aesthetics. He thinks that the most elementary procedure of art is "to substitute for the object its image."[49] Not its concept: a concept is "the object grasped, the intelligible object."[50] The image, once presented, declares its independence; it does not even pretend to obey the syntax of reason or intelligibility. Instead, it exerts its power by force of magic, imposing itself upon us as a distinctive rhythm or semblance. If reasons and causes appear in a work of art, they have no other purpose than to produce a certain cadence; they are spells and chants. So far as I enter upon a work of art, I consent to its rhythm, and am drawn into what Levinas calls "a participation."[51] I am carried away, along a passage from myself to anonymity. The aesthetic element is sensation, and its time is "the meanwhile." Levinas is bound to suspect art because it blurs the distinction between one subject and another, I and Thou, upon which ethics depends. It consorts with states of feeling and sensation in which we find ourselves playing a role in a drama that has begun outside of us. When Levinas speaks of art, he cites with rebuke the post-Romantic terminologies which have been devised to indicate the force of art without designating its character or accounting for it: genius, inspiration, intoxication, the unconscious, magic, myth, ecstasy, transcendence, the sacred, the sublime, mysticism, Pure Poetry. It is a scandal to Levinas that a work of art changes discourse into incantation.[52]

Not surprisingly, Levinas prefers to write about philosophers rather than about artists. With philosophers, he can argue, and argument is enough. With artists, he can argue, but he knows that argument is beside the aesthetic point. With an artist whom he is compelled to admire—Dostoevsky, Proust, Leiris, Blanchot—he tries to find a point of confluence at which his own philosophic judgment is confirmed. In the essay on Proust, Levinas finds the interiorization of the Proustian world troubling: it arises "from the very structure of appearances which are both what they are and the infinity of what they exclude." Proust turns the soul into an outlaw, featuring "a compossibility of contradictory elements, and a nullification of every choice." So far, a rebuke can hardly be avoided. But at the eleventh hour Levinas saves the Proustian situation by finding in it a determinate doubleness, compatible with I and Thou:

In spite of Lachelier's principle, which distinguishes between grief and reflection on grief, the one being grievous, the other merely true or false, Proustian reflection, which is governed by a sort of refraction, a gap existing between the ego and its state, puts its own stress on the inner state. Everything takes place as if the self were constantly doubled by another self, with a friendship that cannot be matched, but equally with a cold strangeness that life struggles to overcome. The mystery in Proust is the mystery of the other.[53]

In Proust, it is not the inner event as such that counts, "but the way in which the self seizes it and is bowled over by it, as though it were encountered in another." On Marcel's love of Albertine, Levinas says that Proust situates reality "in a relation with something which forever remains other, with the Other as absence and mystery, in rediscovering this relation in the very intimacy of the 'I'." Strangely, Levinas does not explicitly assure us that the relation discovered in the very intimacy of the "I" is not a mere alter ego, a mere shadow of oneself, but he implies as much when he says that Marcel "did not love Albertine, if love is a fusion with the Other, the ecstasy of one being over the perfections of the other, or the peace of possession." Whatever Marcel feels for Albertine, it must be protected against the dire temptations of "fusion," "ecstasy," and "possession." Levinas makes this clear in a passage about solitude and the breakdown of human communication, the distresses commonly deemed to be the worst obstacles to universal brotherhood:

> But if communication bears the marks of failure or inauthenticity in this way, it is because it is sought as a fusion. One begins with the idea that duality must be transformed into unity, and that social relations must culminate in communion. This is the last vestige of a conception that identifies being with knowledge, that is, with the event through which the multiplicity of reality ends up referring to a single being and where, through the miracle of clarity, everything that encounters me exists as coming from me. It is the last vestige of idealism.[54]

The relation of lover to beloved, as Levinas says in *Totality and Infinity*, should be one of respected distance: "it does not fill the abyss of separation; it confirms it."[55]

III

J. M. Coetzee's *Age of Iron* (1990) is a novel that might have been written under Levinas's auspices.[56] Set in Capetown in 1986, it is a letter from Mrs. Curren to her daughter, a young woman who has cleared out of South Africa ten years ago and vowed never to return till those responsible for the regime of apartheid are "hanging by their heels from the lampposts." She is living a comfortable middle-class life with her husband and their two children in the United States. Mrs. Curren starts writing the letter on the day after she has learnt from Dr. Syfret that she is dying; her cancer is painful and incurable. On the same day, a few hours later, she finds, in the alley behind her garage, a house of carton boxes and plastic sheeting and a man curled up inside. She recognizes him as a derelict, a man of the streets, a beggar, a drunkard, "unclean." She shouts at him and he goes away. But he comes back. She gives him food. In return, he spits on the concrete beneath her feet: "his word, his kind of word, from his own mouth, warm at the instant when it left him." To whom this writing, Mrs. Curren asks? "The answer: to you but not to you; to me; to you in me." (6)

Is there a Levinasian question of fusion here? There is a question, but Mrs. Curren is not guilty of idealism in Levinas's terms. We recognize a distinctive cadence in the movement of her sensibility. She tries for a word or a phrase, then questions it, steps back from its claim, refines it, and adds other phrases to clarify what she means, taking and giving: "his word, his kind of word, from his own mouth, warm at the instant when it left him." That's as much as she can do to get the spit right. So with the letter to her daughter, as if to say: "it is to you, yes, but in other respects it is not to you but to me." Trying again, it is as if she wrote: "it is to the you in me, the quasi-American part of me but not that alone." The letter is not a soliloquy pretending to be a letter; it is an examination of conscience, a confession, technically addressed "to you but really to the you who is also in me." Trying further, as if to say: "I am not immune to the values that have sent you flying off to safe, rural America, even if in days ahead I denounce you for leaving me."

So the letter proceeds. Mrs. Curren tells how she takes the derelict—Mr. Vercueil—under her care; how she tries to help her housekeeper Florence and Florence's son Bheki. She doesn't claim to be heroic, but we make the claim for her. A lesser person would have handed Vercueil over to the police. Perhaps she feels she has been complicit with apartheid and its Afrikaner regime and is belatedly turning liberal. I doubt it. Her behavior toward Vercueil, Florence, and the other "wretched of the earth" is spontaneous, primordial. No theory has preceded it. She acts before thinking. She puts herself at risk, challenges the police and the law, goes far out of her way to help Bheki and his friend John. These people are strikingly unattractive, sullen, graceless: they call on Mrs. Curren to help but they don't speak a word of thanks when she risks her life for them. When she protests to Florence, in an oppressed moment, "I cannot turn my home into a haven for all the children running away from the townships," Florence says, "But why not?" leaning forward. "Why not?" It is the leaning forward, not just the insistent question, that testifies to the conditions that Mrs. Curren has to put up with. She puts up with them. But she can't bring herself to like the people she befriends. She hides John from the police, not because she loves him but because it is the decent thing to do. She writes to her daughter:

> I do not love this child, the child sleeping in Florence's bed. I love you but I do not love him. There is no ache in me toward him, not the slightest.
>
> Yes, you reply, he is not lovable. But did you not have a part in making him unlovable?
>
> I do not deny that. But at the same time I do not believe it. My heart does not accept him as mine: it is as simple as that. In my heart I want him to go away and leave me alone.
>
> That is my first word, my first confession. I do not want to die in the state I am in, in a state of ugliness. I want to be saved. How shall I

be saved? By doing what I do not want to do. That is the first step: that I know. I must love, first of all, the unlovable. I must love, for instance, this child. Not bright little Bheki, but this one. He is here for a reason. He is part of my salvation. I must love him. But I do not love him. Nor do I want to love him enough to love him despite myself. (136)

Meanwhile she is dying and makes only one request: she asks Vercueil to post the letter, after her death.

But there is one episode in the novel that would make Levinas tremble. Three pages before the end, Mrs. Curren tells her daughter that she has been shuffling through the photographs she has sent from America over the years, and looking especially at one in which the two grandsons are in a canoe on a lake. They are wearing orange life-jackets, "like water wings of old":

Why is it that this material, foreign to me, foreign perhaps to human-kind, shaped, sealed, inflated, tied to the bodies of your children, sig-nifies so intensely for me the world you now live in, and why does it make my spirit sink? I have no idea. But since this writing has time and again taken me from where I have no idea to where I begin to have an idea, let me say, in all tentativeness, that perhaps it dispirits me that your children will never drown. All those lakes, all that water: a land of lakes and rivers: yet if by some mischance they ever tip out of their canoe, they will bob safely in the water, supported by their bright orange wings, till a motorboat comes to pick them up and bear them off and all is well again. (194–195)

This outburst recalls a much earlier passage:

It is the roaming gangs I fear, the sullen-mouthed boys, rapacious as sharks, on which the first shade of the prison house is already begin-ning to close. Children scorning childhood, the time of wonder, the growing time of the soul. Their souls, their organs of wonder, stunted, petrified. And on the other side of the great divide their white cousins soul-stunted too, spinning themselves tighter and tighter into their sleepy cocoons. Swimming lessons, riding lessons, ballet lessons; cricket on the lawn; lives passed within walled gardens guarded by bulldogs; children of paradise, blond, innocent, shining with angelic light, soft as putti. Their residence the limbo of the unborn, their innocence the innocence of bee grubs, plump and white, drenched in honey, absorbing sweetness through their soft skins. Slumbrous their souls, bliss-filled, abstracted. (17)

The good life in Capetown and the other good life in America. The later passage ends with a retraction, to some degree, but not enough to remove the venom from Mrs. Curren's letter:

Do I wish death upon my grandchildren? . . . By no means do I wish death upon them. . . . No, I wish your children life. But the wings you have tied on them will not guarantee them life. Life is dust between the toes. Life is dust between the teeth. Life is biting the dust.

Or: life is drowning. Falling through water, to the floor. (195)

Again the triple cadence: Life is A, then B, then C, dust the motif that holds them together, the sub-motif the alliterative "between . . . between . . . biting."

What can we make of these un-Levinasian outbursts? Un-Levinasian, because Levinas would not allow Mrs. Curren to exclude, to denounce, to repudiate. Nor would he tell her that her grandchildren, like the cocooned white children in Capetown, are all God's children and to be treasured equally for that reason. He would tell her that each of them is another person, the Other embodied. Who is Mrs. Curren to say what Life is, as distinct from what a particular life is? Yes, she is at the end of her tether, and at the end of the rope of words that ties her and her daughter. She is exasperated by the "interinanimation"—it is Donne's word—of their lives and wants to put the distance of rebuke between them. She has had enough of "to you but not to you; to me; to you in me." She wants to be rid of everything in her life except Vercueil, who can't swim, can't fly, hasn't learnt to love. The letter, like the life, ends:

I got back into bed, into the tunnel between the cold sheets. The curtains parted; he came in beside me. For the first time I smelled nothing. He took me in his arms and held me with mighty force, so that the breath went out of me in a rush. From that embrace there was no warmth to be had. (198)

I revert to the ethical turn in criticism. Is there any merit in it? Levinas's books and essays tell us how we should live. We should live by prose, have nothing to do with poetry, music, art, rhythm, the lure of imagery. We should maintain lines of demarcation, clarity, avoid imprecision, sublimity, intoxication, being driven beyond ourselves. I suppose it is good to be admonished in this way, but it is also absurd. Levinas says: Thou Shalt Not Commit Murder. But *Macbeth* is neither enhanced nor disabled by that commandment. A work of literature does not consist of lives transcribed; it consists of lives imagined and brought severally to the condition of form. Form is the making of sense among the lives. *Age of Iron* is a novel, a work of fiction, it imagines certain lives and brings them together in conflict and embarrassment. It does not tell readers how to live, what to do; it asks them to imagine what it would be like to be Mrs. Curren, to be Vercueil, Bheki, Florence, Mrs. Curren's daughter, a cocooned child, a boy with an orange life-jacket in a canoe. Reading is an act of attention. The time it takes to read *Age of Iron*—but it takes more than time—is time one sets apart for paying attention. I enter the words and live among them. I imagine what it would be to be someone else. I imagine this not in a condition of sky-blue freedom and detachment, but subject to many forces, some of them extraneous. Levinas's ethics may be one such force, if we let it be heard, but it is only one: it has to make its way against other forces, some of them pressing but trivial. It is a force while the reading lasts and for an indefinite time thereafter, perhaps for five minutes or for the rest of one's life. There is no telling.

What of poetry, mysticism, the lure of rhythm, and the other forces that Levinas holds in suspicion? They seem to me to survive his form of attention intact. Think of all the sentient life we value precisely because it eludes definition and demarcation: states of wonder, ambiguity, susceptibility to chance, the luck of being alive in our moment. As for poetry: a poem of Baudelaire's or of Eliot's is what it is, its life is—in Susanne Langer's term—virtual; it is offered only to be perceived. We are not instructed to live as J. Alfred Prufrock may be thought to live, but only to perceive that imagined life and to hold it in our minds as a thing to be perceived. The poem has no further design upon us; though to let it have any design upon us, we have to submit ourselves to its rhythm—Levinas's word for danger—at least for the time being.

CHRIST AND APOLLO

MANY YEARS AGO, WHEN I WAS TEACHING AT THE HARVARD SUMMER
School, I met Allen Tate, a poet, novelist, and critic I had long admired.
I don't recall our conversation, except that he urged me to read a book
by Father William Lynch called *Christ and Apollo*. I had read three or four
of Father Lynch's essays on theology and the literary imagination, but
none of his books. When I read *Christ and Apollo*, I saw why Tate thought
well of it: the philosophy of imagination it expounded coincided with
his own. Tate's understanding of literature is given in several essays but
most clearly in two, "The Symbolic Imagination" and "The Angelic
Imagination," and the gist of it is in the first of these. "The Symbolic
Imagination" starts as a meditation on Canto 33 of Dante's *Paradiso*, con-
centrating on the imagery of mirrors and wheels—

> A l'alta fantasia qui mancò possa;
>   ma già volgeva il mio disio e 'l velle,
>   sì come rota ch'igualmente è mossa,
>   l'amor che move il sole e l'altre stelle[1]

—and it goes on to adumbrate a philosophy of symbolic action. Dante's
imagination in the *Paradiso*, Tate says, is "an action in the shapes of this
world: it does not reject, it includes; it sees not only with but through the
natural world, to what may lie beyond it." The quality of this image "is wit-
nessed by its modesty." It never "begins at the top; it carries the bottom
along with it, however high it may climb."[2] The symbolic imagination

"conducts an action through analogy, of the human to the divine, of the natural to the supernatural, of the low to the high, of time to eternity." The poet must do his work, Tate says, with the body of this world, "whatever that body may look like to him, in his time and place—the whirling atoms, the body of a beautiful woman, or a deformed body, or the body of Christ, or even the body of this death." If the poet is able "to put into this moving body, or to find in it, a coherent chain of analogies, he will inform an intuitive act with symbolism; his will be in one degree or another the symbolic imagination."[3]

Tate was instructed in these relations by Maritain's books, especially *The Dream of Descartes.* His reading of Dante was also illuminated by Charles Williams's *The Figure of Beatrice* and H. Flanders Dunbar's *Symbolism in Mediaeval Thought and Its Consummation in The Divine Comedy.* Maritain clarified for Tate another form of imagination which they called angelic and agreed in deploring. The angelic imagination resents the limitation of being human, Tate says, it "tries to disintegrate or to circumvent the image in the illusory pursuit of essence." It refuses to look at the natural world, and therefore it sees nothing. Tate takes Poe as an exemplar of this imagination, and finds in his fiction instances of the hypertrophy of the three classical faculties: feeling, will, and intellect. The first hypertrophy is "the incapacity to represent the human condition in the central tradition of natural feeling." The second is "the thrust of the will beyond the human scale of action." The third is "the intellect moving in isolation from both love and the moral will, whereby it declares itself independent of the human situation in the quest of essential knowledge."[4] Poe exhibited all three forms of vanity, but he was not alone in his excesses. Tate maintained, in passing, that modern Catholic poets from Francis Thompson to Robert Lowell had become angelic, had lost "the power to start with the 'common thing,'" the "gift for concrete experience."[5] Catholic poetry in that respect did not differ from poetry by Anglicans, Methodists, Presbyterians, and atheists. I interpret Tate as saying that angelism is the post-Cartesian form of pride.

It is also a sign of historical and religious loss. Tate recalled that poets of his generation had been impressed by Baudelaire's sonnet "Correspondances," "which restated the doctrines of medieval symbolism by way of Swedenborg." According to the sonnet, Nature is a temple, its pillars speak occult words: man moves through forests of symbols that look at him. Perfumes, colors, and sounds answer each to each: "Les parfums, les couleurs et les sons se répondent." There are perfumes as fresh as the bodies of children, mellow as oboes, green as fields: there are other perfumes, perverse, rich, triumphant; they have the expansion of infinite things, which chant the ecstasies of spirit and the senses. Tate reports that he and his colleagues were impressed by Baudelaire's poem "because we had lost the historical perspective leading back to the original source."[6] But he might have noted that the original source was not free of dispute.

Auerbach's essay "Figura" explains that there were two rival Christian traditions of interpretation. One, represented by Tertullian, insisted on the literal and historical validity of the Old Testament and claimed that it was not diminished by figural interpretation: the figure had just as much historical reality as the events it adumbrated and prophesied. The other, represented by Philo and Origen, "strove to transform the events of the New and still more of the Old Testament into purely spiritual happenings, to 'spirit away' their historical character." It was Augustine who ensured that the literal and historical emphasis would prevail: "his thinking was far too concrete and historical to content itself with pure abstract allegory."[7] But when the tradition of figural interpretation lapsed, there was nothing left to sustain the finite image and to give it the enabling power it had in Dante. Angelism is another name for spiritualism.

These few remarks are perhaps enough to indicate the context of *Christ and Apollo*. Lynch takes Apollo to stand for literature in its proud, intransigent capacity, when it scorns the world and insists on the infinite freedom of Kierkegaard's "aesthetic man." He has an interest in submitting Apollo to the greater virtue of Christ:

> On the other hand I mean Christ to stand for the completely definite, for the Man who, in taking on our human nature (as the artist must) took on every inch of it (save sin) in all its density. . . . I take Him, secondly, as the model and source of that energy and courage we again need to enter the finite as the only creative and generative source of beauty.[8]

Lynch holds that the literary imagination should be a cognitive passage "through the finite and definite realities of man and the world." Those realities are primarily the human body, time, place, society, ordinary life, and its culmination in death. Where Tate speaks of the symbolic imagination, Lynch speaks of the analogical imagination. Referring to the fourfold medieval system of interpretation or the four levels of insight—the literal, the moral, the allegorical, and the analogical—Lynch argues that there is finally only one—the literal—"which has been brought to complete illumination by the minds marching through all its possibilities."[9] Christ is the supreme paradigm in body, time, and world. Indeed, Lynch nearly says that if we sufficiently ponder the life of Christ in the world and the radiance of it, we hardly need to trouble ourselves with God in any other capacity. The finite, literal image is enough, if we consider it under the auspices of analogy. As Lynch says, "the Catholic imagination does not force me to imagine that at the end I must free myself from all human society to unite myself with God." Rather, he says, "it helps me to imagine that once I have embarked on a good thing with all its concreteness (here it is society), I can and must carry it with me all the way into the heart of the unimaginable."[10] A motto for this emphasis, I suggest, is available in Paul's epistle to the Ephesians:

> Wherefore he saith, When he ascended up on high, he led captivity captive, and gave gifts unto men.
>
> (Now that he ascended, what is it but that he also descended first into the lower parts of the earth?
>
> He that descended is the same also that ascended up far above all heavens, that he might fill all things.) (4:8–10)

But I have some questions. I understand why Lynch is opposed to the prejudice of late-nineteenth-century French poetry in its Mallarméan bearings, its determination to seek the essence of a thing at whatever cost to the thing itself: the essence of a flower when every trace of its texture, color, and smell has been sublimed away—the flower absent from all bouquets, as Mallarmé says. Lynch deplores Pure Poetry and the motives that keep it going. He prefers Hopkins's "The Wreck of the Deutschland" to Eliot's "Little Gidding" for that reason. But I wonder whether his philosophy of the imagination doesn't commit poetry to the limited purposes of description, designation, and reference. Blake attacked Wordsworth for capitulating to the natural world, and he insisted on the privilege of imagination—which he called vision—in its most peremptory character. There are moments, especially in the three versions of *The Prelude,* when Wordsworth appears to yield to Blake and puts the natural world in second place. But generally he incurred Blake's resentment. I find that Lynch would bring an Act of Uniformity to bear upon writers, as he does in his strictures on Camus, Graham Greene, Eugene O'Neill, and Eliot. He does not concede to them what Henry James called their *donnée* or their chosen ways of engaging with their concerns. He is not, indeed, a literary critic. He gains access to a work of literature only so far as the designation of themes and characters goes. He has little or no sense of literary form, of the difference that formal aspiration makes. Baudelaire, Flaubert, Proust, and Eliot appear in Lynch's book as if they were journalists who have to be rebuked for not fulfilling the principle of analogy.

I I

But there is a more difficult consideration. In Lynch's book, as in Tate's essays, the force of analogy is invoked, but it is not explicated sufficiently for my needs. "Analogy," Lynch says, "is a metaphysical explanation of the structure of existence, indeed of all that exists."[11] It may be, but I fear those big words. My questions begin further back. What, as precisely as possible, is analogy? Is it a cognitive act? Analogists seem to be doing something other than knowing or exploring. Is analogy an exact mode of knowledge, or knowledge so weak that it is merely a conventional recognition of similarity? Perhaps it is a narrative or structural development of likeness. In *L'Etre et les êtres* Maurice Blondel says that analogies are based "less on notional resemblances (*similitudines*) than on an interior stimulation, an assimilative solicitation (*intentio ad assimilationem*)."[12] But who intends, who solicits? Is analogy an attribute of one's mind or of the world at large? Does it always take the form: as such-and-such is the case, so also is a different such-and-such the case? As cause is to effect, so is heat to melting wax, to cite one of Kant's instances? In the *Nicomachean Ethics* Aristotle says that you have to be a lyre-player, to start with, before you can become a good lyre-player, so also you have to be a man before you can become a good man. Is that an example of analogical thinking? Bewildered, I have been impelled to do a little homework and to begin, where many of these ladders apparently start, with Aquinas. Not that he ever wrote a treatise on analogy, but he often referred to it and gave his sense of it in passing. I gather that most students of analogy have taken their bearings either from Aquinas or, in a different tradition of thought, from Kant. According to Kant, analogies are rules which must govern all appearances of objects in the same objective time. These rules are empirical, not transcendental; they apply only to objects of a possible experience, not to things-in-themselves. They don't lead from the empirical to the transcendental. The relations that obtain in Kant's analogies are all on the same cognitive level: cause and effect, substance and accident. He doesn't help, if you want to intuit a something-else beyond the finite image. Lynch, Tate, Maritain, and Blondel add footnotes to Aquinas. I don't think they engage with Kant's epistemology at any point. I'll try to bring together the considerations of analogy that arise from *Christ and Apollo*.

I assume that analogy is a necessary device because there is no special language to refer to the supernatural or indeed to spirituality. We have no prose for God. We have only whatever words we use to refer to our bodily presence in the world, our sensory knowledge, and reflections on those experiences. When we try to go beyond these limits, we merely use ordinary words with a different inflection. We say "spirit" in a different tone of voice as if it were independent of body, but it still means breath, no matter whose breath we intend. We want to transcend our expressive and linguistic constraints. Analogy seems to arise when we feel impelled to say something, for one reason, and know that we can't say it adequately, for another: it arises from the pressure of constraint, limitation, paradox. Or, as E. L. Mascall puts it more judiciously:

> The doctrine of analogy is not concerned to discover whether discourse about God is antecedently possible, or to endow it with a possibility that was originally absent, but to account for the fact that discourse about God has, as matter of experience, been taking place

in spite of various considerations that might seem at first sight to
rule its possibility out of court.[13]

But that doesn't say anything about the quality of our discourse about
God, or guarantee that it won't be specious. Such discourse may be hap-
less in every referential sense, but even if it is, it may still express our
desires and needs, like cries in the dark. Or it may have its value in
another mode. To say that "God is merciful" does not make the same
claim as to say that "Judge Scalia is merciful," because we can't know that
God fulfils our concept of justice as Judge Scalia does or does not.

Etienne Gilson has made the point that such a statement about God
has no merit if we speak it in the order of the concept; but it acquires
merit if we speak it in the order of the judgment:

> We must observe, in fact, that in the case of God, every judgment,
> even if it has the appearance of a judgment of attribution, is in
> reality a judgment of existence. When we speak, with reference to
> God, of essence or substance or goodness or wisdom, we are doing
> nothing more than repeating about Him: he is *esse*.[14]

But Gilson doesn't make us take a vow of silence. Following Aquinas,
he says:

> Every effect of God is analogous to its cause. The concept which we
> form of this effect can in no case be transformed for us into the
> concept of God which we lack, but we can attribute to God, by our
> affirmative judgment, the name that denotes the perfection corre-
> sponding to this effect. To proceed in this way is not to posit God
> as similar to the creature, it is to ground oneself on the certitude
> that, since every effect resembles its cause, the creature from which
> we start certainly resembles God.[15]

How distant the resemblance is, there is no need to say. It follows, in
Mascall's terms, that "analogy does not enable us to *conceive* God's good-
ness as identical with his essence but to *affirm* it as identical with his
existence." Hence, as Mascall maintains, "all our assertions about God

are grossly inadequate in so far as they apply concepts to him, but they are thoroughly adequate in so far as they affirm perfections of him."[16] But Mascall's argument seems to me an awkward one. Gilson says that whatever statements we make about God, they all come down to an affirmation of His existence. But Mascall evidently wants us to be able to say laudatory things about God without talking nonsense. The problem is that this device could be used by someone who hated God—Vasili Rozanov or William Empson, for instance—and wanted to affirm in Him perfections of evil. I don't see any way of getting around this embarrassment. If we are believers and place ourselves in the orthodoxy represented by Tertullian, Augustine, and Aquinas, then analogy makes speech about God available to us, however inadequately. We don't have to talk nonsense and we can maintain a principled reserve: we know that the gaps are immeasurable, they can't be filled with syntax, but they may be leaped—if we want to leap them-by invoking edifying paradigms of likeness and proportionality. Aquinas holds that two things are analogous because one "receives its intelligibility from the other." The analogy of the creature to its Creator is of this type:

> The creature has existence only insofar as it descends from the First Being and it is called a being only insofar as it imitates the First Being. The same thing holds for wisdom and all the other perfections which are predicated of the creature.[17]

Presumably Aquinas would regard perfections of evil and malice as mere lacks, deficiencies, absences of good: negations.

I have assumed that the speech of analogy is sacramental. Something is deemed to be itself and at the same time a sign of something else. Paul writes, in his first letter to the Corinthians:

> The cup of blessing which we bless, is it not the communion of the blood of Christ? The bread which we break, is it not the communion of the body of Christ?
>
> For we being many are one bread, and one body: for we are all partakers of that one bread. (10:16–17)

"Communion" receives its intelligibility from "bread." The "body" makes kinship with the body of Christ in senses literal, moral, allegorical, and analogical.

But this doesn't seem quite right; it makes analogy belong not only to the sacramental but to the semantic order. Until better instructed, I hold that analogy is an experimental or heuristic rather than a cognitive act: it seems to be a play of similitudes, not of identities. The ground of it is a community of intelligibles which can be correlated without filling in the syntactical gaps: it is enough that the intelligibles so associated make instances of likeness, proportion, and exemplarity. Mind and the things it thinks of; Creator and creatures; substance and accidents; potency and act; cause and effect: we can juxtapose these paired considerations without inserting a copula between them.

In some cases the use of analogy has been effective politically and legally. If you start with the eternal being of God, it is easy enough to go from that to the continuous being of certain institutions, the papacy, for instance. Popes die in their natural bodies, but the papacy does not die. Ernst Kantorowicz has shown, in *The King's Two Bodies*, that the theological concept was soon given a worldly correlative. The king has two bodies: one of them is just as mortal as anyone else's, the other is a corporate or symbolic body that does not die. Legally, General Motors does not die with the death of its CEO. During the past forty years or so, some historians have been studying the political consequences of the distinction, in consideration of the power of God, between *potentia dei absoluta et ordinata*, power absolute and power ordained. Theologians from the early thirteenth century on have pondered what God could do and what He has chosen to do. Is the absolute power of God presently active, or does it refer to "the total possibilities *initially* open to God, some of which were realized by creating the established order" while the unrealized possibilities "are now only hypothetically possible"?[18] The issue was not confined to the question of Christ's power, as son of God, in working miracles. Francis Oakley has pointed out that the distinction was invoked not only in theology but in epistemology, natural philosophy, ethics, and civil law. The *potentia dei absoluta* was called upon, he says, "to assert the possibility of our having intuitions of non-existing objects; to facilitate the pursuit of speculative possibilities pertaining to notions of infinity, the void, and the plurality of worlds; to underline the utter dependence of moral norms on the mandates of the divine will; and by analogy to make the point that although the prince (imperial no less than papal) should indeed live and discharge his duties in accordance with the law, he was not bound to do so out of necessity."[19] A prince who so acted did so out of benevolence: he could just as freely have chosen to act above or aside from the law. Normally the analogical sequence started with considerations of divine power, but it went the other way, too. Descartes moved from reflecting on the power of an absolute monarch to the conviction that God could have changed the laws of mathematics if he had wanted to and could have ordained that twice four would not be eight.[20] It was common to claim that God's relation to the world is analogous to that of a sculptor to his statue; but that claim has been objected to on the grounds that "the causal relation asserted between God and the world *cannot*, in principle, be identical with that between sculptor and statue."[21] Analogy has also been useful for persuasive purposes in politics. If a state wanted to evoke respect and obedience in its citizens, it could recite the analogy of a father to his children, with an implication that the values came from natural law. Feminists are quick to note that the analogy is never based on a mother's relation to her children.

I I I

It begins to appear that analogical thinking may be strict or loose: strict if it sticks to the point, the relation apprehended, and works through it in respectably severe terms; loose if it grasps at the merest straw of likeness. So the question of analogy and metaphor regularly arises. Lynch maintains that analogy and metaphor are not the same. He rejects the claim that "metaphor is the very heart of poetic structures." The force of the analogy of being is, he thinks, endless, but "metaphor may be the last and the least of the forms of the imagination." This is a strange position to take. I'm aware that some scholars in the past twenty years or so have been undermining the Aristotelian privilege of metaphor as the crucial act of the poetic imagination. Paul de Man, J. Hillis Miller, and other writers have proposed to set up the figure of prosopopoeia in place of metaphor: prosopopoeia is the figure by which one summons an absent person to come forth, a ghost to appear and speak. The reason for dislodging metaphor in favor of prosopopoeia is to void the claim of stability apparently enforced by the relation of likeness: if you claim that one thing resembles another in some respects, you stop the play of differences for the time being. You make the world appear to be stable. Prosopopoeia makes no such claim. It acts only locally and says nothing about being or relations. It is the speech act that brings a semblance of something into being, rather than the speech act that says that one thing is so like another as to assume its identity, however implausibly. But Lynch's dismissive account of metaphor is not in the service of prosopopoeia, it has a different aim. He argues that "a metaphor, no matter what its power, is that kind of 'same but different' relation to another thing in which the same can be quite clearly blocked off from the different":

> My God may very well be a mighty fortress, as the Lutheran hymn declares, but we also know very well that He is not a mighty fortress. Whereas when the Catholic analogist says that he knows with his mind and from his mind that God has a mind, he is not at all saying, despite the infinite differences, that it is of course also clear that God does not have a mind.[22]

Lynch goes on to claim that "*action* is the soul of the literary imagination in all its scope and forms, and that metaphor either springs out of action as one of its finest fruits, or is itself one of its many forms." I think he has in mind Aristotle's statement that a tragedy is an imitation of an action, and Francis Fergusson's interpretation of action as meaning something like our word "motive." The action of *Hamlet* is the deliberate motive it enacts, to root out and destroy the evil that is corrupting the state of Denmark. When the motive is largely unconscious, as it is in *Macbeth*, it acts not from deliberation but in response to certain images of power; passion undermines or usurps the rights of reason. In *The Human Image in Dramatic Literature* Fergusson takes as motto of this violence Macbeth's claim, after he has killed Duncan's murderers: "Th' expedition of my violent love/Outrun the pauser, reason." (II.iii.115–116) Lynch's point seems to be that action is prior to the figures it uses, and that metaphor is merely one of these figures, not a privileged one.

But Lynch's reasons are hard to follow. I'm shocked to hear that a Catholic would infer from the fact that he has a mind that God has a mind. God is not a person merely because I am a person. Aquinas says: "'Person' is said of God and creatures neither univocally nor equivocally but analogously. . . . It is said antecedently (*per prius*) of God, then of creatures."[23] I've assumed that sound analogical thinking goes from Creator to creature but not from creature to Creator. It starts from the creature in the sense that that's the only thing I can know, but when it deduces the Creator from the creature, it immediately acknowledges that the Creator is, as Aquinas says, First Being. Even if I am an effect, I am not justified in claiming that God as the cause is cognate to me, or even the perfection of my imperfect being. The fact that I have a mind doesn't entitle me to say that God has a mind, even a mind to the nth degree of mine.

On the question of analogy, Lynch apparently thinks that the same and the different are simultaneously active in the object or event: to see it as the same, you look at it from one angle, to see it as different you look at it from another. No doubt. But it doesn't follow that the same in metaphor can be clearly blocked off from the different. John Crowe Ransom's "The Equilibrists" involves the notion that the lovers are separate planets whirling past each other. Empson has interpreted many of Donne's love poems as saying, or having the lovers claim, that they together make a separate planet, and are therefore exempt from the puny laws of Earth. The lovers are not a planet, in sober fact, so in that sense the same can be clearly blocked off from the different, but they feel themselves to be as united in their love as if they constituted a separate planet. That feeling, since we are reading poems rather than consulting astronomical charts, blurs the epistemological distinctions and makes it not at all easy to block off the same from the different. The several poems are different modes of the relation between feeling and form.

But I should look into the question of metaphor more closely. Lynch evidently thinks that analogy is adequate, as if by definition, to whatever reality it addresses and that metaphor is merely an enabling rhetorical figure like any other. I find myself thinking that what he regards as a defect in metaphor, I regard as one of its glories. If someone feels old, dispirited, sees himself getting bald, and feels otherwise a bit Prufrock-ian, he might say—

> That time of year thou mayst in me behold
> When yellow leaves, or none, or few, do hang
> Upon those boughs which shake against the cold,
> Bare ruin'd choirs where late the sweet birds sang.[24]

It is a merit, not a defect, that these lines commit themselves to the meta-phor—I am a season, declining to the end of the year—stay with it, and put up with its limitation. Of course it would be possible to say to the complainant: your metaphor is fallacious, because we have good cause to think that the year will turn to Spring and new leaves will flourish. The complainant would retort: precisely, life will persist and thrive in another season, but it won't be my life or my season: meanwhile what I feel is the pain of "ruin'd" and the nostalgia of "late." It is precisely the partiality of the metaphor, its inability to be right and adequate all along the experi-ence, that makes it right if not adequate.

Frost's "Nothing Gold Can Stay" deploys a similar feeling along the lines of analogy: it doesn't use a metaphor beyond the first line, where "green" is a synecdoche, a variant of metaphor by which the part stands for the whole: green is a sign of seasonal emergence, richness of renewed being:

> Nature's first green is gold,
> Her hardest hue to hold.
> Her early leaf's a flower;
> But only so an hour.
> Then leaf subsides to leaf.
> So Eden sank to grief,
> So dawn goes down to day.
> Nothing gold can stay.[25]

The method in the first two couplets is discursive; the first line of each states a fact of observation, the next one adds a judgment or a qualification. This procedure changes with the pivotal line, "Then leaf subsides to leaf." The play between green and gold, and between leaf and flower, is stilled by the repetition, leaf to leaf. The tone of the poem responds to the basic grammatical figure of analogy: as such-and-such, so such-and-such. The first "so," in the fourth line, is in a minor key, quiet between "only" and "an hour." But the next "So" is analogically emphatic and has the emphasis of being placed at the beginning of its line; so also the next and last "So," also the first word of its line. The last line makes its sad assertion on the strength of the two "So" lines, the two analogies.

Hugh Kenner has made a pertinent remark on the procedure of this poem. In a handbook of poetry for students he says:

> Do lines 1–5 outline the course of a day or the course of a season? If the former, then the "gold" is merely a trick of early light; if the latter, then it is a phase through which the leaves themselves actually pass. What difference do these possibilities make when we get to line 6? A poem built out of analogies can "prove" nothing; but it can testify to the degree of thought that has preceded its composition.[26]

Kenner's question about line 6—"So Eden sank to grief"—seems to say: the line implies that the Fall of Man, the sin of Adam and Eve, was in the nature of things, just as natural and just as inevitable as the fall of leaves. But, Kenner implies, if the analogy is based on a trick of early light, it's specious, and if it's based on a larger sequence of lapses, it's only a bit less specious. The fact that leaves fall or turn gold tells us nothing about the Fall of Man, but they indicate the degree of thought—not much, he seems to claim—that preceded the composition. Presumably he would say that in Shakespeare's sonnet there is no such defect: the speaker merely says that he feels like a declining season of falling leaves. He doesn't compromise the Fall of Man.

Shakespeare's sonnet seems to know the limits of its metaphor and to live with them. But sometimes a poem will flaunt its metaphor and challenge its readers to say that it's blatantly extravagant. Richard Crashaw's epigram "On our crucified Lord Naked, and bloody" works up its two metaphors, the blood of the crucified Christ as his garment, and his body as a wardrobe:

> They have left thee naked Lord, O that they had;
> This Garment too I would they had deny'd.
> Thee with thy selfe they have too richly clad,
> Opening the purple wardrobe of thy side.
>> O never could bee found Garments too good
>> For thee to weare, but these, of thine owne blood.[27]

The immediate source is Matthew 27:28–31, which is virtually the same as Mark 15:17–20. Here is Matthew:

> And they stripped him, and put on him a scarlet robe.
>
> And when they had platted a crown of thorns, they put it upon his head, and a reed in his right hand: and they bowed the knee before him, and mocked him, saying, Hail, King of the Jews!
>
> And they spit upon him, and took the reed, and smote him on the head.
>
> And after that they had mocked him, they took the robe off from him, and put his own raiment on him, and led him away to crucify him.

Crashaw imagines Christ already crucified, and makes grim but thrilling play with the only garment that remains, his blood, and the wound that opens his wardrobe to let out more of such raiment. Robert Martin Adams's comment is to the point:

> Blood is a royal garment as it is precious, purple, and confers a crown; yet it clothes many souls otherwise naked, hence the wound from which it proceeds is a clothes-closet. Nothing, from one point of view, could be more disgusting and grotesque. Yet how else to convey the combination of sacred, spiritual preciousness with the vulgar,

social utility which is most oddly betrayed by our expression "*Good Friday*"? One may, presumably, feel that it is silly to think about Christ's blood in two such different ways at once; given the objective, it's not clear how one could hit off such a thought more neatly than in a phrase like "purple wardrobe"—though (*because*) in the process decorums wonderfully collide.[28]

I would add that Lynch would have to find Crashaw's metaphors scandalous, if only because they don't allow the same to be blocked off from the different. The colliding decorums scorn the lucidity of such blocking-off. The feeling is precisely the collision, and Crashaw challenges us to refute its intensity.

I V

I think I understand why theologians want to distinguish analogy from metaphor. Analogy is a sober exercise, even though it is claimed to be endless in its resource: it sticks to certain traditional issues, of which the relation between Creator and creature is the most far-reaching, and it abides by a few criteria, including especially likeness and proportionality. Metaphor, as Donne's poems and Crashaw's show, is often wilful and audacious; it prescribes relations, partial indeed, between any two things. If a question of good taste arises, as it did for Robert Martin Adams with Crashaw's epigram, the poet is indifferent to the charge. He claims that the vehemence of his passion requires for expression every reach of exorbitance. He does not keep his decorums in their separate places. These metaphors may have started with analogical propriety, but at some point they seem to have gone wild or frantic. No wonder Lynch wants to keep them in their lowly places.

But a larger question arises. Has the tradition of analogy collapsed? Modern scientists have given up the metaphysical analogy, predicated on Being, in favor of relations predicated on knowledge. They put in brackets the metaphysical relations and appeal to the predictive force of knowing. They often use counterintuitive models, as in basic quantum mechanics and speculative cosmology, but they prefer worldly models—

electrons are like billiard balls. In some instances analogy has taken the social form of Taste. Roberto Calasso has remarked:

> For a number of years after the fall of the "correspondences" (symbolic equivalences—the last canon), a tacit concordance among manners, gestures, and physiologies functioned as law. Although clearly precarious, this silent accord still made a show of being solid, set on an enduring foundation, and obviously more legitimate than every one of its barbarous predecessors.[29]

Tate argued that the symbolic imagination—which as I've indicated was his phrase for the analogical imagination—arose "from a definite limitation of human rationality which was recognized in the West until the seventeenth century; in this view the intellect cannot have direct knowledge of essences." The only created mind "that has this knowledge is the angelic mind." Tate continued:

> If we do not believe in angels we shall have to invent them in order to explain by parable the remarkable appearance, in Europe, at about the end of the sixteenth century, of a mentality which denied man's commitment to the physical world, and set itself up in quasi-divine independence. This mind has intellect and will without feeling; and it is through feeling alone that we witness the glory of our servitude to the natural world, to St. Thomas's accidents, or, if you will, to Locke's secondary qualities; it is our tie with the world of sense.[30]

The moral of Tate's commentary is that so long as people understood the limitations of their minds and that they could not have direct knowledge of essences, they were content to have their minds engage with existence, the finite world, and to go as far as they could with that commitment. Analogy, which offered intimations of likeness and proportionality, did not transcend the limitations of sensory knowledge and reflection; nor did it encourage people to delude themselves into fancying that they could assume the powers of angels. But it enabled people to speak of God and divine things under the accepted shadow of limitation and from the deep resources of their desire. Tate's concern, like Maritain's, is how it came about that this network of accepted limitations broke down in the early seventeenth century and allowed people to think that their minds could indeed have knowledge of essences. Tate says:

> The angelic mind suffers none of the limitations of sense; it has im-
> mediate knowledge of essences; and this knowledge moves through
> the perfect will to divine love, with which it is at one. Imagination in
> an angel is thus inconceivable, for the angelic mind transcends the
> mediation of both image and discourse. . . . When human beings
> undertake this ambitious program, divine love becomes so rarefied
> that it loses its human paradigm, and is dissolved in the worship of
> intellectual power, the surrogate of divinity that worships itself. It
> professes to know nature as essence at the same time that it has
> become alienated from nature in the rejection of its material forms.[31]

The political form of angelism entails revulsion against whatever merely exists and a determination on the part of societies to celebrate themselves, as in the Nuremberg rallies.

We may now ask whether or not this angelic imagination is still the predominant one in modern and contemporary literature. Without having read everything, how could we answer that question? But it is hard to think of writers who work upon the principles of analogy as if those principles were still there to be worked on. Frost's poem "Nothing Gold Can Stay" appears to go through the motions of analogy and uses its procedures: as *this*, so *that*. But Frost is indifferent to the Thomist precision of analogy; he relies on the asserted privilege of his feeling. There are writers of acute religious concern: Walker Percy, Flannery O'Connor, J. F. Powers, Andre Dubus, John Updike. But these writers don't give the impression of supposing as writers—I can't speak of them in their personal commitments—that there is any mediating or enabling expressive force between themselves and their highest aspiration. They think they have to do the whole job by themselves. Analogy is of no help to them.

But the principle of analogy often finds a degree of acknowledgment where you would not have anticipated such a sentiment. Wallace Stevens's essay "Effects of Analogy" starts by identifying analogy with allegory, as in Bunyan's *Pilgrim's Progress* and the *Fables* of La Fontaine. Stevens then notes that analogy is a term in logic, and quotes Susan Stebbing's *Logic in Practice:*

> Inference by analogy consists in inferring that, since two cases are alike in certain respects, they will also be alike in some other respect. For example, since Mars resembles the Earth in certain respects, we infer that Mars also is inhabited. This may be a very risky inference, for Mars differs from the Earth in some respects, and these differences may be relevant to the property of being inhabited.[32]

Stevens regards this sense of analogy as a narrow one, though proper to logicians; he is not bound by it. He thinks of analogy, in poetry and criticism, as a principle of likeness, according to which "the nature of the image is analogous to the nature of the emotion from which it springs." Matthew, in his gospel, says that Christ went about the cities, teaching and preaching, and "when he saw the multitudes, he was moved with compassion on them, because they were scattered abroad, as sheep having no shepherd." The analogy between men and sheep, as Stevens says, "does not exist under all circumstances":

> There came into Matthew's mind in respect to Jesus going about, teaching and preaching, the thought that Jesus was a shepherd and immediately the multitudes scattered abroad and sheep having that particular in common became interchangeable.

Of the Greek poet Leonidas's lines—"Even as a vine on her dry pole I support myself now on a staff and death calls me to Hades"—Stevens says:

> The particular is the staff. This becomes the dry pole, and the vine follows after. There is no analogy between a vine and an old man under all circumstances. But when one supports itself on a dry pole and the other on a staff, the case is different.[33]

More generally:

Take the case of a man for whom reality is enough, as, at the end of his life, he returns to it like a man returning from Nowhere to his village and to everything there that is tangible and visible, which he has come to cherish and wants to be near. He sees without images. But is he not seeing a clarified reality of his own? Does he not dwell in an analogy?[34]

So in "To an Old Philosopher in Rome" Stevens thinks of Santayana living out his last years in a convent in Rome, and he imagines him dwelling in an analogy—

> The threshold, Rome, and that more merciful Rome
> Beyond, the two alike in the make of the mind.[35]

In the make of Santayana's mind, to begin with, and then in Stevens's mind, by sympathetic attention. I don't claim that Stevens was precise or rigorous in his dealings with analogy: he often took it to mean mere likeness, as many of us say "analogously" when we merely mean "similarly." Stevens practiced analogy only in secular or naturalized forms, bringing into relation not one image and another, but an image and the emotion—someone's emotion—from which it springs. In his poems, analogy is a psychological relation between a mind and its favorite images; they are favorite images because of the feelings they gratify.

I have not forgotten Eliot. Lynch gives a brief and notably severe comment on *Four Quartets:* the poet has failed, apparently, to live up to the imperatives of analogy. Quoting several short passages from the *Quartets,* Lynch says that in these "the Christian imagination is finally limited to the element of fire, to the day of Pentecost, to the descent of the Holy Ghost upon the disciples":

> The revelation of eternity and time is that of an *intersection,*
>> But to apprehend
>> The point of intersection of the timeless
>> With time, is an occupation for the saint—

It seems not unseemly to suppose that Eliot's imagination (and is not this a theology?) is alive with points of *intersection* and of *descent*. He seems to place our faith, our hope, and our love, not in the flux of time but in the *points* of time. I am sure his mind is interested in the line and time of Christ, whose Spirit is in his total flux. But I am not so sure about his imagination. Is it or is it not an imagination which is saved from time's nausea or terror by points of intersection?[36]

Lynch complains that Eliot does not find value and significance in human life as such, in the continuous flux of it, its latitude. What he mostly feels is the nausea of temporal existence. A second complaint emphasizes the first: it is that Eliot's poetry does not endorse the privilege of action, it does not register human life as a continuous drama, alive in every moment. My own view is that for Eliot, as for any Christian, the Incarnation is the supreme intersection of the timeless with time. But I agree with Lynch that Eliot's imagination is not constitutionally analogical; it finds value in the intense moment, the epiphany, but not in "the waste sad time stretching before and after." Time is there only to be redeemed, Eliot believes, and it can be redeemed only by recourse to a higher perspective, a pattern exempt from mere temporality. When Eliot's imagination tries to retain the finite image while reaching beyond it, it seeks Dante's companionship, needing this guidance, this intercession, to stay in communion with the requisite analogies, even at a distance. At the end of "Little Gidding," it is by recourse to Dante that Eliot can imagine the condition in which "the tongues of flame are in-folded/Into the crowned knot of fire/And the fire and the rose are one."[37]

Eliot's example and Stevens's indicate that at least some of the resources of analogy are still available, by allusion. The tradition of analogy as a form of thinking, alive from the Church Fathers to the seventeenth century, retains intermittent life: there are signs of it in Lawrence's *Women in Love* and Golding's *The Inheritors*. The method is allusion, but that is not a disability. Allusion is the method of nearly every significant reference. Pound's *Cantos*, Olson's *The Maximus Poems*, Joyce's *Ulysses* and *Finnegans Wake*, and Eliot's *The Waste Land* allude to other times, other cultures, and point to values they had that we lack. Allusion is always possible, but there are many forces working against analogy. The most assertive of these is the widespread repudiation of myth—or of metanarrative, to use Lyotard's word—of any story that testifies to life as such, or to particular lives in the aspect of their shared meaning. Frank Kermode's *The Sense of an Ending* is the most eloquent denunciation of myth: inevitably, it speaks up for fictions, which are deemed to have the merit of being consciously false and therefore to have no designs on our behavior. Myths are now deemed to be corrupt, they supposedly issue from a gross totalizing ambition. Every system is said to be a system of power, raging to impose itself. So it is not surprising that the literary fragment is claimed to be the only form without guilt.

Another force working against analogy is the charge that it is complicit with the Aristotelian-Thomist rhetoric of identity, presence, and substance. Gilles Deleuze makes this charge in *Différence et Répétition*. John Milbank has taken up the issue in *Theology and Social Theory*, where he concedes to Deleuze, to begin with, that "if analogical predication applies only at the level of *genera*, and across the categories of substance and accident, in such a fashion that the substantial is the 'basic' meaning, to which the accidental is referred, then this suggests a hierarchical convergence towards a literal 'sameness' of being, which is the presence of God."[38] Milbank is complaining, apparently, that in Aristotle and Aquinas analogy goes from the privileged term to the secondary one. Substance is primary, accident secondary. The 'same' is primary, 'difference' secondary. I don't understand how it could be otherwise. If the Creator is First Being, everything else must be secondary. Milbank, having conceded so much to Deleuze and to other Nihilists, as he calls them, goes on to argue that "the critique of presence, substance, the idea, the subject, causality, thought-before-expression, and realist representation does not necessarily entail the critique of transcendence, participation, analogy, hierarchy, teleology and the Platonic Good, reinterpreted by Christianity as identical with Being."[39] But the price is high: it entails giving up the Aristotelian-Thomist categories. Milbank says that "analogy does not imply 'identity,' but identity and difference at once, and this radical sense can be liberated if one jettisons the genera/species/individuals hierarchy and recognizes, *with* the nihilists, only mixtures, *continua*, overlaps and disjunctions, all subject in principle to limitless transformation." But we don't need this liberation. I don't see why, to make the point that analogy implies identity and difference at once, you have to jettison Aristotle and Aquinas: analogy, in the scholastic tradition, acknowledges identity-and-difference at once, just as metaphor does. Milbank then offers another gift I have never longed for. When the Aristotelian-Thomist categories are abandoned, he says, "then the way is open to seeing analogy as all-pervasive, as governing every unity and diversity of the organized world." In regard to the analogy of beings to Being, "such a mode of analogy would be divorced from *pros hen* predication, in so far as this gives priority to substance, because God would no longer be the subject of the 'proper,' literal application of the analogical quality, but simply the infinite realization of this quality in all the diversity and unity of its actual/possible instances."[40] I would like to be clear about this. Milbank wants to retain the principle of analogy, but to separate it from its traditional interpretation in terms of Aristotle and Aquinas. He seeks "a Christian theological equivalent to Heidegger's temporalizing of Being." In that form, I suppose it might be compatible with Lynch's project, and Tate's: the process of analogy, in Milbank's phrasing, is "our participation in divine Being, now understood as a participation also in the divine creativity which reveals itself as ever-new through time."[41] But Milbank seems to be of two minds here. He accepts analogy as a capacity of Being, but he is ready to give up—in favor of 'difference'—the primary designation of Being as the principle embodied in substance, the 'same,' and identity. I don't know whether or not he is prepared to abandon the metaphysics of Being, as Levinas, Habermas, and Rorty are, each for his own reasons.

V

Christ and Apollo was not Father Lynch's last word on the subject. Ten years later, in 1970, he published *Christ and Prometheus*, taking Prometheus to represent the secular project. Prometheus stole fire from the gods, gave it to mankind, and Zeus punished him for his transgression. *Christ and Prometheus* asks: "How can we restore an inner unity to the divided religious imagination of our day, racked as it is by living in a narrow religious corner and a huge secular world?"[42] Lynch's answer is surprising. You would have expected him to attack the secular project for its meanness of spirit, its application of energy and power to the transformation—and often the exploitation—of the natural world and defenseless people. You would have thought he would deplore the insistence of the secular project for the bewilderment it causes, but he doesn't. He gives it more than its due, insisting on its proper autonomy. He praises it for refusing to find meaning outside its own processes. In a word, he reconstrues the project in such a way as to take the harm out of it and leave the worldly good of it intact. He hopes to reconcile Christianity and the Enlightenment by making each of them better than its ordinary self. He wants the secular work to persist but to act from its best self, freed of mechanism and abstraction. Equally, he wants Christianity to know its best self. Lynch wrote *Christ and Prometheus* against the belief, evident in some religious thinkers, that the secular and the sacred were one and the same. The message of Dietrich Bonhoeffer, John Robinson, Friedrich Gogarten, and other such minds was: take the mystery out of Christianity and set it to work in the world. These people, Lynch said, "would settle for a little Christ over against a great if purified Prometheus." He will have none of it. The sacred, he says, "must reassert itself in its own right and refuse at all cost to be dissolved into anything other than itself." To do that, it needs a new "image of secularity" within which it can live, breathe, and work. Conflict then becomes unnecessary. Perhaps Lynch makes the situation a little easier by saying that "the sacred is *par excellence* the inner life, the absolute self-possession and self-identity of God." Prayer is its outward sign. There is a slight implication that "the sacred" has a better chance of surviving if it keeps itself to itself. But the moral of Lynch's story—the relation between these two books—is quoted from a passage in Whitehead's *Adventure of Ideas:* "I hazard the prophecy that that religion will conquer which can render clear to popular understanding some eternal greatness incarnate in the passage of temporal fact."[43]

BEYOND BELIEF

THE TITLE OF ROBERT BELLAH's *BEYOND BELIEF* IS TAKEN NOT FROM the common phrase but from a poem by Wallace Stevens called "Flyer's Fall." We are to think of a flyer falling to his death, flying into nothingness, as Stevens writes—

> Profundum, physical thunder, dimension in which
> We believe without belief, beyond belief.[1]

Bellah says of those lines:

> Had he stopped with "We believe without belief," we might have understood him simply as some stoic existentialist trying to make the best of a world he never made. But "beyond belief" shows that the symbolism, unavoidable though it is, is not final but only provisional. Our "central men" will go on giving us ever new conceptions of the whole, which, though fictional and provisional, will take us ever deeper into the mystery of being.[2]

Bellah apparently doesn't see how empty those last words are—"ever deeper into the mystery of being." The phrase has lost the hope that may once have animated it: wherever Stevens's phrase takes us, it is not deeper into the mystery of being. Besides, there is an equivocation in those lines of Stevens's poem. The profundum, the physical thunder, may be the object of our belief, that to which we give our assent for what it's worth;

or, more likely, it may be the space, the dimension, in which we practice living without belief, in the hope of going beyond belief into some other experience. In Dublin many years ago I attended a lecture by Gabriel Marcel in which he made a distinction, which he later developed in a book justly called *The Mystery of Being*, between "belief in" and "belief that." "Belief that" is the assent one gives to a sequence of propositions, without considering the moral quality of the person who has declared them: one deems them to have impersonal authority and takes them as true. "Belief in" is the assent one gives to a person or a god, a commitment that does not depend upon propositions or axioms but upon one's saying yes to that person or god. If I believe in someone, I trust her, I open an unlimited account in her favor. Jesus may have gathered apostles and disciples around him by the cogency of his statements, but it is more probable that they committed themselves to him in response to his force of presence. They said yes to him before he had said much to them, they did not wait for the logic of his concepts. Then there is the further sense of belief according to which we believe someone or we believe God, the fullness of our belief being the avowal of it. It is not quite the same as "belief in." The object of "belief in" may also be something that exists independently of us; as we say that an artist believes in his work or his genius. What lies beyond belief is hard otherwise to say. Stanley Cavell says of Beckett's characters that "their problem is not to become believable, but to turn off the power of belief altogether since it has become, because useless, the source of unappeasable, unbelievable pain." Instead of saying "Lord, I believe; help thou my unbelief," they say: "Help me not to believe."[3]

Bellah's *Beyond Belief* has a chapter on Stevens, whom he regards as a fellow-spirit and as "the greatest American 'theological poet' of the twentieth century."[4] I admire Stevens's poetry, but I don't understand the sense in which he is said to be a theological poet, unless Bellah has in view—as I'm afraid he has—some form of secular theology which is designed to get rid of theology. But the question is worth looking into before coming to Bellah and the sociology of religion. Stevens normally used the word "belief" in the sense of "belief that." "What am I to believe?" he asks in "Notes toward a Supreme Fiction." Sometimes he used it to mean a state of feeling in which we stand ready to believe something, as distinct from the more pervasive state in which we assure ourselves that we do not believe anything. He rarely wrote of "belief in," though the security of his common style indicates that he believed in himself and in his Muse. I don't think he distinguished between several degrees or qualities of "belief that." He didn't mull over the differences between belief, faith, assent, credence, *croyance*, conviction, certitude, and so forth. I don't think he weighed Newman's distinction between notional assent and real assent. Stevens did not need to think of such differences. He assumed that the word "belief" in its ordinary religious usage denoted an impossibility, so it was unnecessary to elucidate the several available degrees of it. I am not referring to Stevens's conversion to Roman Catholicism on his death-bed, an event for which there is adequate evidence. I refer to Stevens only as the author of his published poems and essays. In that capacity he capitulated to what he accepted as the *Zeitgeist* to the extent of saying that we live in a time of disbelief and therefore that belief is impossible. Like Marx, he assumed that the criticism directed upon religion was complete and that, as Marx said, "the task of history, once the world beyond the truth has disappeared, is to establish the truth of this world."[5] Not that Stevens was willing to hand over the task to historians, even to Marxist historians; he determined to take part in it as an amateur epistemologist and a part-time poet. He thought of his poetry as constituting a song of the earth, in counterpoint to Dante's songs of hell, purgatory, and paradise. It did not occur to him to wonder how men and women just as perceptive as himself and living at the same time could commit themselves to Christianity, as a case in point; or how millions of people throughout the world continue to believe in God and to live their lives according to the Christian dispensation, despite Nietzsche's assurance that God is dead and that Christianity is a structure of cowardice, debility, and *ressentiment*. Did Stevens really think that Simone Weil had wasted her life, soul and body, by remaining attentive to every experience of doubt and belief? Should she have taken Nietzsche at his word and devoted herself to worldly pursuits? Did Stevens think that T. S. Eliot was brainwashed on the occasion of being baptised in the Anglican communion in June 1927; or that he was deranged when he wrote, a few months before his baptism, that he believed "that the chief distinction of man is to glorify God and enjoy Him for ever?"[6] In fact, Eliot's understanding of belief was far more complex than Stevens's. Reviewing I. A. Richards's *Science and Poetry*, Eliot said:

> Mr. Richards's faculty for belief . . . suffers, like that of most scientists, from too specialized exercise; it is all muscle in one limb, and quite paralysed in another. When I peruse Mr. [Bertrand] Russell's little book, *What I Believe*, I am amazed at Mr. Russell's capacity for believing—within limits. St. Augustine did not believe more. Mr. Russell believes that when he is dead he will rot; I cannot subscribe with that conviction to *any* belief. Nevertheless, I cannot "believe"— and this is the capital point—that I, any more than Mr. Russell and others of the more credulous brethren, get on for one moment without believing *anything* except the "hows" of science.
>
> Mr. Richards seems to me to be the dupe of his own scepticism, first in his insistence on the relation of poetry to belief in the past, and second in his belief that poetry will have to shift without any belief in the future.[7]

Eliot's dealings with the words "belief," "conviction," "credulous," and "scepticism" in that passage show that he thought about the experiences to which those words refer more pointedly than Stevens did.

But I should not imply that Stevens was indifferent to religion or debonair in the absence of belief. If he were, he would not have spent so much energy and written so many lines to assure himself that all was well and that he was content with his paganism. In the section of "Notes toward a Supreme Fiction" to which I've referred, he answers the question "What am I to believe?" by imagining an angel leaping down "through evening's revelations," but then he asks: "Am I that imagine this angel less satisfied?" Stevens claims that the poetic imagination that imagined the angel is greater than the angel; and, if that is the case, the hour of this imagining is filled "with expressible bliss." If there is an hour in which the poet is satisfied "without solacing majesty," then there is a day, a month, a year, an entire time in which majesty is—and how could it be anything else, given those values?—"a mirror of the self." "I have not but I am and as I am, I am." The allusion to the Book of Exodus and God's statement to

Moses—"I am that I am"—is daring, and quite in keeping with Stevens's determination to replace theology by aesthetics. As for the infinite spaces:

> These external regions, what do we fill them with
> Except reflections, the escapades of death,
> Cinderella fulfilling herself beneath the roof?[8]

It was indelicate of Stevens to direct his irony upon poor Cinderella: many of his own poems are Cinderella-work, familiar with day-dreaming, glass slippers, and midnight fulfillments.

But Stevens's normal device to express the expressible bliss of living without belief, beyond belief, was to take Christian words of faith and vision and translate them downward, reducing them to humanist terms. Hans Blumenberg has argued, in *The Legitimacy of the Modern Age,* that modern secular thought takes its discourse from religion, which it subverts by domesticating its mysteries. Secular thought is rarely as strict in its secularism as it claims to be; its majesty is a mirror of former piety, rejected in principle but persisting through its shadow. Milbank has gone further and maintained that modern sociology is constituted in its secular character by its heretical relation to Christianity. The motto for this procedure is given in Stevens's "Final Soliloquy of the Interior Paramour": "We say God and the imagination are one." The saying is honorable because it doesn't claim more authority than itself. The God named in that line is the God of power: its humanistic version is the poetic imagination in its will to change the world to itself, making consciousness responsible for the whole of its experience. In philosophy, the name for this determination is Idealism, according to which freedom is real only as power, the power to change objects into the one subject, my sole self. Or the semblance of power, seeming to effect this change. In the same spirit, Stevens replaces truths by fictions. A local truth demands to be believed. Stevens rejects the demand, and fills the space of it with fictions of his own devising: these he has no trouble believing, because he has made them. He has evidently been reading Hans Vaihinger's *The Philosophy of 'As If'* and reserving the word "truth" for the experience of enjoying his fictions. Stevens writes:

> The final belief is to believe in a fiction, which you know to be a fiction, there being nothing else. The exquisite truth is to know that it is a fiction and that you believe in it willingly.[9]

"Final" doesn't seem the right word: the main characteristic of these experiences is that in them the poet composes one fiction and then another one, and the fictive process which stops only with one's death is deemed to make up for the arbitrariness of every fiction. Stevens finds the truth of this exquisite, meaning that it is an acute pleasure while it lasts, like decadent poetry. Like "the nicer knowledge of / Belief, that what it believes in is not true." Nice knowledge, nice work. A belief then becomes a sensuous experience of the world by which a vital instinct in the poet is gratified; it is as if he went out-of-doors on a windy morning and felt pleased to be part of the weather and made this pleasure indistinguishable from belief.

Fictions serve many purposes in Stevens's work: they keep his inventive capacity at full stretch, one fiction leads to another, and each is exempt from the irony he would direct against any official proposition or image that offered itself as true. But I can't see how he is justified in claiming to believe in them. If I invent a fiction, I may take pleasure in it, but I can hardly believe in it. A more provisional verb is appropriate. Perhaps I entertain the fiction, play with it, enjoy the elegance of it, take it as a happy notion. But I can hardly give it real assent, knowing that the sole authority it comes with is that I have made it. The experience is pure tautology. It is improper of Stevens to say that he believes something: he changes his belief too soon and too often to deserve the attribute of believing. Promiscuous in these relations, he should say, I surmise or I guess or I have a hunch. I say I believe when I can't honorably say I know.

Stevens not only replaces local truths by his fictions: he replaces the idea of truth by what he calls "a Supreme Fiction," and gives it three qualities: it must be abstract, it must change, and it must give pleasure. In an early poem he says to a devout woman that "Poetry is the supreme fiction, madame," but much later he approaches the Supreme Fiction by making notes toward it, as a musical theme might be approached not by declaring it in advance but by composing variations on it and leaving it to be divined. I need not give a list of Stevens's secular translations. It is not surprising that he reduces "soul" to "self," as in "A Collect of Philosophy" where "the soul lives as the self."[10] Or that he translates love to inspiration, and an ideal loved one to the Muse: "And for what, except for you, do I feel love?"

The purpose of these secular or humanistic reductions is to disable religious belief while preserving its aura. Certain residual satisfactions and consolations ensue. In "Two or Three Ideas" Stevens speaks of the Greek Gods as if anything he might say of them would apply equally to the God of the Old Testament and the God of the New. He reports the death of these gods, one and all, and for a while allows a mild sense of loss to darken his sentences:

> In an age of disbelief, or, what is the same thing, in a time that is largely humanistic, in one sense or another, it is for the poet to supply the satisfactions of belief, in his measure and in his style. . . . To see the gods dispelled in mid-air and dissolve like clouds is one of the great human experiences. It is not as if they had gone over the horizon to disappear for a time; nor as if they had been overcome by other gods of greater power and profounder knowledge. It is simply that they came to nothing. Since we have always shared all things with them and have always had a part of their strength and, certainly, all of their knowledge, we shared likewise this experience of annihilation. It was their annihilation, not ours, and yet it left us feeling that in a measure we, too, had been annihilated. It left us feeling dispossessed and alone in a solitude, like children without parents, in a house that seemed deserted, in which the amical rooms and halls had taken on a look of hardness and emptiness.

At this point Stevens takes a breath and sets out toward the predictable satisfactions of humanism. The death of the gods is absolute, he claims: his tone is that of "Sunday Morning," in which he allows for the persistence of the desire to believe while voiding the object of belief:

> What was most extraordinary is that they left no mementos behind, no thrones, no mystic rings, no texts either of the soil or of the soul. It was as if they had never inhabited the earth. There was no crying out for their return. They were not forgotten because they had been

part of the glory of the earth. At the same time, no man ever mut-
tered a petition in his heart for the restoration of those unreal shapes.
There was always in every man the increasingly human self, which
instead of remaining the observer, the non-participant, the delin-
quent, became constantly more and more all there was or so it seemed;
and whether it was so or merely seemed so still left it for him to
resolve life and the world in his own terms.[11]

These sentences are so handsome that I am reluctant to deride their as-
sertions. But it is hard to take them seriously as an account of the pagan
gods, the Christian God, and the beliefs they provoke. "The increasingly
human self" is a value diminished by Stevens's insistence on it. The im-
pingements of belief and disbelief, over a period of centuries, can't be
reduced to such a cartoon. It is easy enough to explain the broad strokes.
Stevens wanted a religion without belief or practice; he wanted to rid
himself of the doctrines while enjoying a trace of them in his sensibility;
so he retained their figures and metaphors, enriching his poetry by hav-
ing it crossed with images and shadows of divine things. But he would
not submit himself to beliefs and observances he had not invented.

The main problem with Stevens's procedures is that he seems to
achieve his ends at little cost. When we think of Beckett's characters as
Stanley Cavell has described their predicament, or when we think of
Melville's wrestlings with God, or of Dostoevsky's grand inquisitions, we
are bound to feel that it cost Stevens comparatively little to live without
belief or to move beyond it. "Without" and "beyond" come too easily to
his mind to make us care about the sequence: no pain darkens it. If you
can translate "God" as "the imagination" and effect the translation as
swiftly as Stevens did, you are not spilling real blood or crying bitter
tears. It is not true that, as Schiller wrote, "when the gods were more
human, human beings were more like gods."[12]

I I

It is not surprising that Bellah quotes Stevens in a book on "religion
in a post-traditional world." He evidently thinks that Stevens, more than

any other writer, articulates a religious sensibility that sustains itself without belief and aspires somehow to go beyond belief in a direction that can't be indicated. In *Beyond Belief* Bellah admits "that science can never wholly take over the job of making sense of the world,"[13] and he concedes that religion may have something to say about the opacities of human life. But you would never discover from his books what religion is, apart from the empty formulae of his gestures toward it. Nor would you discover how religion has come to be dark with mystery. Bellah takes religion to be whatever it has been in China, Japan, India, Italy, or anywhere else: it is "that symbolic form through which man comes to terms with the antinomies of his being."[14] Religion, according to this lowest common denomination of it, has no necessary involvement with belief. Bellah thinks that "the effort to maintain orthodox belief has been primarily an effort to maintain authority rather than faith."[15] A dubious claim: if an individual makes herself available to the grace of faith, it cannot be for the purpose of gaining authority: she does not acquire any authority by that submission. In other essays Bellah says that the purpose of religion is to provide people with what he calls an "identity conception" in conditions of anxiety, hope, and fear: "It is precisely the role of religion in action systems to provide such a cognitively and motivationally meaningful identity conception or set of identity symbols."[16] In another version, religion is "a control system linking meaning and motivation by providing an individual or a group with the most general model that it has of itself and its world."[17] Again, religion is "a set of symbolic forms and acts that relate man to the ultimate conditions of his existence."[18] But Bellah has no concern for religion except in its social or civic consequence. "Ultimate conditions" do not arise. *Beyond Belief, Habits of the Heart, The Broken Covenant,* and *The Good Society* show that he is indifferent to religion, except as a social institution with some bearing on public order.

Part of the problem is that Bellah is apparently content to use words in such a way as to empty them of their content, especially their doctrinal and historical content. Conceding that social science does not have all the explanations, he proceeds as if it did: he does this by giving such a simplified account of the question of religion that the answer is obvious. He is not alone in these simplifications. Sociologists from Durkheim and Weber to Talcott Parsons have interested themselves in religion as a sentiment that exerts a certain integrative force in society: you would not learn from their books that a history of religion includes Augustine, Pascal, Jeanne d'Arc, Teresa of Avila, and Hopkins. Bellah reduces religion to a few vocables, recites the most commonplace parts of its vocabulary in secular translation, settles upon a few standard images, and offers to endow them with an aura not of sacredness but of utility. With the blindness of his capacity, he speaks of Christianity as if it had nothing to do with mystery, the soul, sacrifice, the holy, sacraments, the Eucharist, or the Trinity. He never doubts that the conditions of religious practice can be comprehended, without defect or distortion, by a sociology of religion. It is not surprising that he looks at religious organizations as "schools of citizenship,"[19] as if religion existed only to turn people into good middle-class bourgeois liberal Americans. He is interested in "civil religion" to the extent to which he finds such a thing active in contemporary America. In *The Broken Covenant* he describes civil religion as "that religious dimension, found I think in the life of every people, through which it interprets its historical experience in the light of transcendent reality," but he has nothing to say of that light, nor is he embarrassed, as he should be, by the lightheartedness of "transcendent" in that last phrase. These are mere gestures. The religion he cares about or offers to understand has even less content than the rudimentary system of belief that Rousseau called "civil religion."

Civil religion, as Bellah uses the term, is an organized sentiment devoid of doctrine or other force. It is low-church Protestantism made still more palatable by the rationalism of the Enlightenment. The clearest account of it in Bellah's writings is a famous early essay, "Civil Religion in America," where he argued not only that there is "an elaborate and well-institutionalized civil religion in America" which exists "alongside of and rather clearly differentiated from the churches" but that this religion "has its own seriousness and integrity." It is recognized as having "a set of beliefs, symbols, and rituals." At its best, he claims, it is "a genuine apprehension of universal and transcendent religious reality as seen in or, one could almost say, as revealed through the experience of the American people." There is much talk of America as the modern version of God's Israel. Bellah quotes with approval de Tocqueville's statement that the religion of the American people is "a form of Christianity which I cannot better describe than by styling it a democratic and republican religion."[20] He has nothing to add to de Tocqueville's description of it, and qualifies it only by saying that the American civil religion is not "in any specific sense Christian." It is related to Christianity but doesn't coincide with it. Bellah is not concerned with those instances—Martin Luther King, Jr., was one—of a politics in direct relation to Christian belief and practice; presumably because a religion, more often, has political consequence only in local communities and their practices.

One of Bellah's examples of civil religion is John F. Kennedy's inaugural address of January 20, 1961. President Kennedy used the word "God" three times in that speech, twice at the beginning and again at the end. At the beginning he said:

> We observe today not a victory of party but a celebration of freedom—symbolizing an end as well as a beginning—signifying renewal as well as change. For I have sworn before you and Almighty God the same solemn oath our forebears prescribed nearly a century and three quarters ago.
>
> The world is very different now. For man holds in his mortal hands the power to abolish all forms of human poverty and to abolish all forms of human life. And yet the same revolutionary beliefs for which our forebears fought are still at issue around the globe— the belief that the rights of man come not from the generosity of the state but from the hand of God.

At the end of the speech, Kennedy said:

> With a good conscience our only sure reward, with history the final judge of our deeds, let us go forth to lead the land we love, asking His blessing and His help, but knowing that here on earth God's work must truly be our own.[21]

Bellah takes those last gestures as providing "a transcendent goal for the political process." I am afraid the word "transcendent" comes too readily to his mind and leaves again without having incited Bellah to any fear or trembling. Kennedy, according to Bellah, is accepting "the obligation, both collective and individual, to carry out God's will on earth." How the President can suppose he knows what God's will is, or how it can be deemed to be carried out by military action in Cuba and Vietnam, Bellah does not say. It is an easy slide from saying that God's work must truly be our own to assuming that our own work coincides with God's will. Civil religion does not resist its being put to mundane political purpose.

Bellah glances at a possible interpretation of the references to God in Kennedy's speech; he doesn't agree with the interpretation, but he concedes that it might be deduced from the words. The passages quoted might be taken to reveal, he says, "the essentially irrelevant role of religion in the very secular society that is America." It might be claimed "that the very way in which Kennedy made his references reveals the essentially vestigial place of religion today":

> He did not refer to any religion in particular. He did not refer to Jesus Christ, or to Moses, or to the Christian church; certainly he did not refer to the Catholic church. In fact, his only reference was to the concept of God, a word that almost all Americans can accept but that means so many different things to so many different people that it is almost an empty sign. Is this not just another indication that in America religion is considered vaguely to be a good thing, but that people care so little about it that it has lost any content whatever?[22]

Bellah disagrees with that interpretation, mainly because he holds that Kennedy's religious beliefs and his relation to the Roman Catholic Church were an entirely private matter, "not matters relevant in any direct way to the conduct of his public office." He continues:

> Others with different religious views and commitments to different churches or denominations are equally qualified participants in the political process. The principle of separation of church and state guarantees the freedom of religious belief and association, but at the same time clearly segregates the religious sphere, which is considered to be essentially private, from the political one.

Bellah's use of the word "sphere," with its implication of a clearly desig-
nated entity that can easily be separated from other spheres, prevents
him from acknowledging that in certain circumstances the issues in reli-
gion and in politics are not at all separable. Kennedy's opponents argued
that his being a Roman Catholic was a political disqualification, a view
they did not succeed in pressing. But the separation of the religious
sphere from the political one, to which Bellah refers, is a much more diffi-
cult proceeding than he recognizes in his talk of two spheres. The legality
of abortion, the question of the provision of abortion services from pub-
lic funds, assisted suicide, same-sex marriage, prayers in public schools,
capital punishment, the concept of a just war: these and many other issues
can't easily be relegated to different spheres.

The constituents of civil religion in America, according to Bellah,
include a theologically vague and unexacting invocation to God, the sharing
of national holidays—Memorial Day, Thanksgiving Day—and the recog-
nition of certain nationally edifying places and artifacts—Gettysburg
National Cemetery, Arlington National Cemetery, the Lincoln Memorial,
the Tomb of the Unknown Soldier. Perhaps he would add the flag, the
National Anthem, and the Vietnam War Memorial. He evidently values
these to the extent of thinking that they amount to a religion good
enough for social and political purposes. He may be right, within the
limits of his interests. He is not alone in looking for a few values that can be
recommended to every citizen of the United States and even to resident
aliens in the hope of instilling in them a sense of their identity as Ameri-
cans. Nor is he alone in thinking that the many rhetorical devices in favor
of diversity and pluralism should be modified by equally cogent school-
ing that emphasizes the family, local groups, and an unemphatic kinship
and unity of purpose. In that spirit Bellah favors a set of vaguely held
beliefs—or rather, inclinations—which are so undemanding that they
could not cause much dissension. With that aim in mind, he employs
strategies that are like Stevens's: he takes certain concepts of religion,
drains off their doctrinal force to the point at which they become almost
entirely secular, and then tries to endow these few concepts with an aura
of political fervor, a secular version of the sacred. The only criterion to be
invoked is the value of these artifacts and practices in bringing people
together as Americans and keeping them together. Easy references to

God, obeisance to the flag, singing the National Anthem at sporting events, the community spirit of football, baseball, basketball, occasional church-going as a domestic custom: these are typical constituents of the American civil religion, religion without doctrine. Of course if you want to call such a loose assemblage of habits a religion, you are free to do so. You may even think of them as making an informally established religion, corresponding to the Anglican Church in the United Kingdom though far more dilute in its theology. It is the established church of the United States in the sense that the Constitution forbids the establishing of any other.

Bellah thinks of civil religion as serving the aims of the nation. It does this by keeping its citizens mindful of the community in which they participate. But in *Beyond Belief* and *Habits of the Heart* the sense of such a community is remarkably feeble: its existence is hardly more than nominal. Not surprisingly, the dominant value in the United States is found to be individualism; either utilitarian individualism, in which each citizen aims to make as much money as possible, consistent with allowing everyone else to do the same; or expressive individualism, according to which people of similar inclination gather into small groups—which Bellah calls "lifestyle enclaves"—to further and enjoy the felicities of that style. Under either of these forms of individualism, the notion of a community is inevitably a distant and chimerical sentiment. Moral issues are judged by their consequence in feeling; if the proposed course of action feels good—or if I feel comfortable with it—it's fine; if not, not. Civil religion brings sweetness of disposition to enhance these purposes. This set of sentiments then takes upon itself the lineaments of the patriotism it resembles.

In *Habits of the Heart* Bellah and his colleagues report the results of their interviews so blandly that it is hard to feel that serious issues are at stake. Here is a typical paragraph:

> The American pattern of privatizing religion while at the same time allowing it some public functions has proven highly compatible with the religious pluralism that has characterized America from the colonial period and grown more and more pronounced. If the primary contribution of religion to society is through the character and con-

duct of citizens, any religion, large or small, familiar or strange, can be of equal value to any other. The fact that most American religions have been biblical and that most, though of course not all, Americans can agree on the term "God" has certainly been helpful in diminishing religious antagonism. But diversity of practice has been seen as legitimate because religion is perceived as a matter of individual choice, with the implicit qualification that the practices themselves accord with public decorum and the adherents abide by the moral standards of the community.[23]

The limitation of Bellah's understanding of religion comes through in virtually every phrase of this passage. His reference to "the primary contribution of religion to society" shows that he can't think of religion in any other terms: it makes a contribution to society, it clarifies the moral standards of the community. Bellah has no idea of a religion that might set itself deliberately to keep its distance from the pieties of politics, or to render to Caesar the things that are Caesar's and to God the far more demanding things that are God's. He does not allow himself to see that a religion might feel impelled to dissent from a particular national program and might try to show it up as sinful. Even more, a religion might put itself at odds with the state by imagining the Good as an alternative to imagining Power.[24] Or it might accuse the civil religion of trying to displace true religion by claiming to pursue similar social purposes more concessively. Bellah doesn't want to think of such activities. He wants to show that politics offers the most comprehensive account of human life in practice, just as social science offers the most comprehensive account of it in theory. At that level of ambition, Bellah's sociology is what Valéry called politics, "the art of preventing people from minding their own business."[25] Religion in any form is supposed to accept a minor role.

Bellah takes lightly the subordination of religion to politics and sociology, for two reasons. He is indifferent to the creeds of any particular religion—he counts them as six of one and half-a-dozen of the others—and he cares only for the civil religion that yields to politics and sociology. The sociology of religion, as he conducts it, is like the Arminian heresy: theology and doctrine don't matter, only good works matter. It follows that the sentiment of democratic politics is encouraged to displace the

potentially divisive force of religious belief and practice. A crisis arises for
Bellah only when there is palpable discrepancy between American for-
eign policy and the inclinations of democratic politics; as, during the
years of the Vietnam War, there was discrepancy between the White
House and the civil religion practised by the Youth Movement and stu-
dents from Berkeley to Columbia.

I I I

The question arises: why call this civil religion a religion? Why not
call it what it is, politics in its practice and civics in its theory? It can't be
anything else, it can't be a serious religion, because Bellah has no time
for faith, revelation, mystery, sacrament, theology, or sacrifice. The only
meaning he respects or claims to respect is social meaning. This makes
the difference between Robert Bellah and David Walsh when they are
considering much the same evidences. David Walsh is a Roman Catholic
and a political scientist. In *The Growth of the Liberal Soul* he argues that
modern liberalism has gained a wide consensus of support by avoiding
unnecessary conflicts and giving an uncontested account of its founda-
tions. But the consensus, he maintains, is unstable so long as liberal con-
victions are not deemed to be sustained "by a larger spiritual impulse."
His thesis is "that liberal resilience is to be attributed to the presence of a
profound spiritual impulse that has remained, despite the disturbances,
as the still point of the turning external world." His main evidence for
this is that "there is a palpable aura of the sacred surrounding certain lib-
eral expressions of the transcendent dignity of the person that call for
the characterization as religious or quasi-religious." A few paragraphs
later, Walsh is ready to attribute this "aura of the sacred" to Christianity:
"liberal order is the trace of Christianity in a world from which it has
withdrawn":

> The legions of Christians, churched and unchurched, should not be
> underestimated in any assessment of the inner resources of liberal
> order. . . . So long as the liberal convictions have not become a substi-

tute for the Christian faith, so long as they do not function as a substitute religion, then there is nothing derivative about their status as a secular reflection of Christianity. It is only when the line between the two is blurred and politics masquerades as religion that an artificial hybrid results. Then the effect is patently contrived and is held together only by the resort to subterfuge and force. Yet the experience of such quasi-religious movements, in the great revolutionary ideologies, should not cloud our sensitivity to the subtler manifestations of the religious spirit in the more moderate development of liberal order. . . . Just as Christianity is in some fundamental sense the truth of the liberal conception, so liberal order can be considered the political truth of Christianity.[26]

It seems to me that Bellah's civil religion is precisely politics masquerading as religion—President Kennedy's invocations to God in the inaugural speech having a bearing on this masquerade—and while I praise David Walsh for clarifying the pretense, I find myself wondering why he is so concerned to give Christianity this social privilege. Why would he want to claim that Christianity is the theory of which modern bourgeois liberalism is the practice? If Christianity is to be proclaimed, it should not be because it apparently sustains a congenial political ideology, bourgeois liberalism: it has persisted for most of two thousand years without doing so.

Reverting to Bellah: what would his civil religion lose, if he were to call it politics and civics, practice and theory? Even in his version of it, civil religion is indeed in its practice a substitute for Christianity; it is politics instead of Christianity, an enhanced politics in a residual relation to a diminished Christianity. Surely it would be better for him to call it politics and try to do the best he can to explain it in that designation. The slight traces of Christianity which his civil religion exhibits are not worth the labor of retaining. The best that can be said for them is that they testify, in a whisper indeed, to the serious religion they have set aside. Is that a testimony worth giving?

But I should make it clear that I am not objecting to a social scientist who takes an interest in a particular aspect of modern life. I am objecting to his giving the title of civil religion to an ensemble of sentiments that does not amount to a religion at all. More specifically, so long as that ensemble of sentiments is called a religion, it degrades the serious issues of religious belief and practice. To call the Youth Movement in 1968 a religion is to misuse language and degrade religion. I am aware of the common prejudice by which issues of life and death are negotiated only in political terms, where alone they are thought to be worth arguing over. But it is improper to appropriate the vocabulary and idiom of a religion on behalf of a politics and a sociology. I am not saying "hands off!" Many modern writers are concerned with religion even though they are not believers. Yeats made a religion for himself—or thought he did—by attaching motifs of the great religions to the theory and practice of magic. Walter Benjamin, at least intermittently, combined his version of Marxism with several intimations of mysticism. The question of Surrealism meant for him the possibility of countering religious illuminations with profane illuminations, issuing from drugs and other material incentives. Jacques Derrida has been pondering several religious occasions, from the Bible to Kierkegaard and Levinas. These sages are not believers, they are not in communion with a church. We do not find them on their knees. They approach religion and its texts to discover there further ways of thinking and feeling. I have no objection to this. Derrida and René Girard are not appropriating the vocabularies of religion for a vulgar purpose, or, like Bellah, trying to enhance certain social habits and sentiments by calling them religious. When Lawrence writes of "the risen Lord," he does not think of stealing the body of Christ: he is finding yet another way of being alive, or a further degree of being alive.

SEVEN

AFTER VIRTUE

IN *AFTER VIRTUE* AND AGAIN IN *WHOSE JUSTICE? WHICH RATIONALITY?* Alasdair MacIntyre maintains that moral utterance and moral practice in our society are chaotic; that they can be understood only "as a series of fragmented survivals from an older past," and that the "insoluble problems which they have generated for modern moral theorists will remain insoluble until this is well understood."[1] The interminable and unsettleable character of so much contemporary moral debate, he says, "arises from the variety of heterogeneous and incommensurable concepts which inform the major premises from which the protagonists in such debates argue."[2] Those concepts "were originally at home in larger totalities of theory and practice in which they enjoyed a role and function supplied by contexts of which they have now been deprived."[3] People continue to search for "a common stock of concepts and norms which all may employ and to which all may appeal,"[4] but they search in vain, there is no such stock. It follows that "our society cannot hope to achieve moral consensus."[5]

MacIntyre points to several instances of interminable and unsettleable debate: on the concept of a just war, the theory of justice, the theory of rationality, and abortion. In the standard debate on abortion one disputant appeals to the sacrosanctity of human life and the right to further life of the unborn, while another appeals to a woman's right to choose. The word "right" is common to both parties, but it is incorrigible as a means of debate because it does not have a common value in both claims. In the same debate the verb "to choose" is regularly left without an object, but if anyone were to supply the obviously suppressed object and take the claim to entail a woman's right to kill an unborn child, the debate might continue, but it could not be settled in moral theory. It could be settled only in the rough practice of politics: whoever produced the bigger battalions would win.

In the absence of an agreed moral vocabulary, MacIntyre argues, we are left with what he calls "emotivism," "the doctrine that all evaluative judgments and more specifically all moral judgments are *nothing but* expressions of preference, expressions of attitude or feeling."[6] These judgments are regularly advanced as if they were impersonal and there-fore had the force of principle, but they are merely disguised versions of arbitrary preference: the emotivist self has no criteria. In such discourse it is inevitable that truth yields to psychological effectiveness, the only value that counts in a therapeutic culture.

The issues that MacIntyre has discussed in *After Virtue* and *Whose Justice? Which Rationality?* are of acute significance in moral and political theory, but I propose to consider their bearing on an activity with which I am more familiar: the theory of literary criticism. Reading MacIntyre, it is natural to ask whether literary criticism is immune to the chaos of con-cepts and values he describes in moral theory. Have critics an agreed vocabulary, a set of concepts to which they can appeal? It seems natural, too—an instance of salience being at hand—that I should look at the ways in which literary critics use the word "life" with normative intent.

II

In October 1979 Czeslaw Milosz published a short but memorably personal essay called "The Real and the Paradigms," a protest against the "European nihilism" he attributed to Nietzsche and thought of as the air breathed by poets in "technologically advanced countries." The only example he quoted of a poem allegedly given over to such nihilism was Philip Larkin's "Aubade." The poem begins:

> I work all day, and get half-drunk at night.
> Waking at four to soundless dark, I stare.
> In time the curtain-edges will grow light.
> Till then I see what's really always there:
> Unresting death, a whole day nearer now,
> Making all thought impossible but how
> And where and when I shall myself die.
> Arid interrogation: yet the dread
> Of dying, and being dead,
> Flashes afresh to hold and horrify.

"Flashes" erupts upon a scene not only dismal but defeated: "afresh" holds out a possibility only to see it canceled:

> The mind blanks at the glare. Not in remorse
> —The good not done, the love not given, time
> Torn off unused—nor wretchedly because
> An only life can take so long to climb
> Clear of its wrong beginnings, and may never;
> But at the total emptiness for ever,
> The sure extinction that we travel to
> And shall be lost in always. Not to be here,
> Not to be anywhere,
> And soon; nothing more terrible, nothing more true.

The logic clicks into place, closing off any further possibilities. The sequence ("Not . . . ," "Not . . . ," "Nothing . . . ," "Nothing . . ." is animated only by the still bleaker "And soon."

> This is a special way of being afraid
> No trick dispels. Religion used to try,
> That vast moth-eaten musical brocade
> Created to pretend we never die,
> And specious stuff that says *No rational being*
> *Can fear a thing it will not feel*, not seeing

> That this is what we fear—no sight, no sound,
> No touch or taste or smell, nothing to think with,
> Nothing to love or link with,
> The anaesthetic from which none come round.

The doomed colloquialism ("none come round") appeals to anyone's sense of life without caring much whether the appeal appeals or not:

> And so it stays just on the edge of vision,
> A small unfocused blur, a standing chill
> That slows each impulse down to indecision.
> Most things may never happen: this one will,
> And realisation of it rages out
> In furnace-fear when we are caught without
> People or drink. Courage is no good:
> It means not scaring others. Being brave
> Lets no one off the grave.
> Death is no different whined at than withstood.

"Chill" inevitably finds its rhyme in "will," an assertion that doesn't need to be made. The future tense is as insistent as the past:

> Slowly light strengthens, and the room takes shape.
> It stands plain as a wardrobe, what we know,
> Have always known, know that we can't escape,
> Yet can't accept. One side will have to go.
> Meanwhile telephones crouch, getting ready to ring
> In locked-up offices, and all the uncaring
> Intricate rented world begins to rouse.
> The sky is white as clay, with no sun.
> Work has to be done.
> Postmen like doctors go from house to house.[7]

Milosz regarded "Aubade" as "a high poetic achievement" and said that "if excellence is an ultimate criterion," the poem "should be unreservedly approved." But then he asked: "is artistic excellence an ultimate criterion?"

Why should I be dissatisfied with this poem? Does it not present our human condition? Does it not cope with the eternal subject of death in a manner corresponding to the sensibility corresponding to the second half of the 20th century? Does not every one of us think of the inescapable end of his or her life, perhaps in a month, a year or two? And yet the poem leaves me not only dissatisfied but indignant, and I wonder why myself. Perhaps we forget too easily about the centuries-old mutual hostility between reason, science, and science-inspired philosophy on the one hand and poetry on the other? Perhaps the author of the poem went over to the side of the adversary and his ratiocination strikes me as a betrayal? For, after all, death in the poem is endowed with the supreme authority of Law and Universal Necessity, while man is reduced to nothing, to a bundle of perceptions, or even less, to an interchangeable statistical unit. But poetry by its very essence has always been on the side of life. Faith in life everlasting has accompanied man in his wanderings through time, and it has always been larger and deeper than religious or philosophical creeds which expressed only one of its forms.

Milosz is already caught up in the idiom of life, "faith in life," life eternal, life everlasting, as if he hoped to clinch a value by repeating it:

> The Psalms of David are poetry of life—even though those who composed them saw the end of man as a pit, Sheol. Somehow a hope of life eternal and a fear of Sheol contradict each other, creating a tension in the Psalms which is one of the secrets of their power.

Milosz scolds Larkin for not participating in the vitalities available to anyone, apparently, who cares to apprehend them:

> The philosophy voiced by the poem of Larkin treats human energy opposing death as a vain consolation. The narrator and hero of the poem is isolated from these energies, forces active in the universe, be they divine or human, and is imprisoned in his ironic self-consciousness. And what would William Blake have to say, were he brought to life and shown "Aubade"? What would Walt Whitman

have to say? These two poets I consider the focal points of energy in the West at the early stages of the scientific-industrial revolution. What a change there has been since their time. As for myself, I hope that I have resisted in my poems that death-wish which disguises itself as an 'objective' constatation of the facts.[8]

No one will presume to question Czeslaw Milosz's indignation, or doubt its authenticity. But his understanding of poetry and his reading of Larkin's poem are askew. He evidently thinks that there is something called Poetry as distinct from particular poems and particular poets, and that he can identify it and speak in its name. By its essence, he claims, poetry has always been "on the side of life, " it has been impelled by "faith in life everlasting": it is larger and deeper than religious or philosophical creeds. Larkin has betrayed this high cause and gone over to the enemy.

But surely Larkin is himself a poet and therefore a constituent of whatever Milosz means by Poetry. Milosz has talked himself into the awkward position of demanding that poets endorse his own faith, his particular sense of life and death. Is artistic excellence "an ultimate criterion," he asks? Apparently not, he implies; though if that is the case, the excellence he ascribes to Larkin's poem becomes a small thing, hardly more than the skill of assembling rhyming words and putting them in a feasibly rational order. It is like having to count up to twenty and getting it right. I have read Milosz's essay several times and I find myself wincing when I come to the claim that "poetry by its very essence has always been on the side of life." I don't believe that poetry has an essence, or that there is such a thing as essential poetry or an essential poem: nor do I think high critical intelligence is compatible with the claim that "poetry" has always been on the side of life. I don't understand how Milosz can claim to know what "life" is and to know when poets and poems are on its side. The facility with which he speaks of the side of the adversary and the side of life is not reassuring. To refer to the Psalms of David as "poetry of life," the genitive being equivocal, makes one doubt that Milosz was prepared on this occasion to work for a difficult sincerity. His reference to "the philosophy voiced by the poem of Larkin" is also misleading. Larkin's poem is not a treatise: what we find in it is a mood, a feeling, but nothing as for-

mulated as a philosophy. And the summary of Larkin's poem as express-
ing a "death-wish" is evidence of a prejudicial reading, the appeal to "life"
being merely a formula, an opportunism.

It would be absurd to make a large claim for "Aubade," or to suggest
that it is one of Larkin's best poems. But it has distinctive merits. It brings
into the scene described far more aspects than the scene would seem to
admit; it opens its predominant mood to larger considerations. And it
does this by discovering certain possibilities among the words:

> In time the curtain-edges will grow light.
> Till then I see what's really always there.

When the curtain-edges grow light, or strengthen in a later formulation,
he will be diverted to see other things, perhaps equally true but not as
compelling as the certainty of his death. "Grow" plays itself off against
the inescapable narrowing of the possibilities, death closing down the
show. "Till then": as if only in the interval of a few hours can he bear to let
his mind be held by the dreadful sense of dying. "What's really always
there"—what's really, when all else is said, a major truth of human life:

> The mind blanks at the glare. Not in remorse
> —The good not done, the love not given, time
> Torn off unused—

What we usually do at a glare is blink, the eyes protect themselves from
the excess of life. Here the mind goes blank, empties itself or lets itself go
empty. The syntactical rhyme of "the good not done, the love not given"
brings these values close, acknowledges them. And then the image of
another page torn out of the calendar, yet another Happy New Year. I
flinch when Larkin mocks religion as "that vast moth-eaten musical
brocade/Created to pretend we never die." Religion is not a pretense. But
the mockery is a sign of Larkin's rage and despair. The poem is valuable
to the extent of its enabling me to imagine what it would be like to feel
like that. I don't ask Larkin to share my feelings, but to give me access to
his, both real and imagined. He gives me access to a quite different range
of feelings on life and death in the last part of "Church Going":

> For, though I've no idea
> What this accoutred frowsty barn is worth,
> It pleases me to stand in silence here;
>
> A serious house on serious earth it is,
> In whose blent air all our compulsions meet,
> Are recognised, and robed as destinies.
> And that much never can be obsolete,
> Since someone will forever be surprising
> A hunger in himself to be more serious,
> And gravitating with it to this ground,
> Which, he once heard, was proper to grow wise in,
> If only that so many dead lie round.[9]

The tone of this differs from "Aubade" mainly because Larkin is willing to acknowledge, as in the Latin of "gravitating," the values explicit in a tradition of moral reflection that has found its way into English.

I take it that "Aubade" is Larkin's reply to William Empson's "Courage Means Running," which speaks of fear as the normal condition of life and of particular crises as intensifications of fear: hence it is "Usual for a man/Of Bunyan's courage to respect fear."[10] Larkin says:

> Courage is no good:
> It means not scaring others. Being brave
> Lets no one off the grave.

But not scaring others—one's children, for instance—is among the best of goods. Of course it doesn't let one off the grave.

The only detail of "Aubade" I regret is the rhyming of "think with" and "link with." The Jerome Kern touch is glib. But for the rest the poem seems to me not a proper object of Milosz's indignation. It imagines—that is, it finds the words to imagine—a feeling neither bizarre nor trivial. The emphasis is not hysterical, though it is familiar with hysteria, as in imagining the telephones crouching, getting ready to ring: getting ready to spring, the verb nearly says.

III

On April 30, 1990, Seamus Heaney delivered one of his lectures as Professor of Poetry at Oxford under the title "Joy or Night: Last Things in the Poetry of W. B. Yeats and Philip Larkin." In effect, Heaney took up the argument where Milosz left it. Again he quoted Larkin's "Aubade," but he went further than Milosz and compared the poem with Yeats's "The Cold Heaven." He did not explain the comparison, apart from saying that in each poem an aging man confronts the thought and image of his death. Yeats wrote the poem in 1912, when he was forty-seven years old and twenty-seven years before his death. But leave that consideration aside. Larkin, or the speaker of his poem, is engaged with the inevitability of his death, the dread of it, the certainty—as he believes—that his death is final. Yeats, or the speaker of his poem, doesn't believe that his death is final. Larkin was an agnostic rather than an atheist, on the evidence of "Church Going" and other poems. "Aubade" is not his last or only word on the question of life and afterlife. He had his moods. Yeats believed in reincarnation—or at least held the idea of it seriously in his mind—and he wrote part of *A Vision* to imagine the forms it might take, the stages he called the Dreaming Back, the Return, the Purification, and so forth. He was sufficiently a residual Christian, a Protestant of an unexacting theological persuasion, to propound an afterlife heterodox indeed but not entirely a scandal to Christians. There is nothing in "The Cold Heaven" comparable to Larkin's dread and fright. The difference between the two poems starts as a matter of different moods in differently moody poets. Neither poet is signing his last will and testament.

Heaney's comparison of the poems is prejudicial. He agrees with Milosz in disapproving of "Aubade," except that he doesn't convict Larkin of being opposed to life. When a poem rhymes, he says, "when a form generates itself, when a metre provokes consciousness, it is already on the side of life." Still, and despite its "heart-breaking truths and beauties," "Aubade" "reneges on what Yeats called the 'spiritual intellect's great work.'" Throughout the essay, Heaney associates "Aubade" with negation and defeatism: it cuts off any possibility of a life after death, and it regards as specious the devices one might resort to—religious belief, courage, work, keeping up one's morale—to challenge the finality of death. But Heaney is not scrupulous in his reading of "Aubade." Before he quotes it in full, he refers to one line of it: "Death is no different whined at than withstood." And he italicizes the *no*, making Larkin say something even more drastic than what he says in the line as printed, where there are no italics and the main emphasis is not on the *no* but on the semantic and acoustic difference between "whined at" and "withstood."

Heaney's vocabulary is telling. He asks whether Larkin's "rejection of Yeats's more romantic stance has not been too long and too readily approved of." His main claim for "The Cold Heaven" is that in it "the poem's stylistic excellence and its spiritual proffer converge":

> When, in one place, the verb 'to quicken' is rhymed with the partici-
> ple 'stricken' and still manages to hold its own against it; and when,
> in another, the rhyme word 'season' sets its chthonic reliability
> against the potentially debilitating force of 'reason'—when such
> things occur, the art of the poem is functioning as a corroboration of
> the positive emotional and intellectual commitments of the poet. To
> put it in yet another and perhaps provocatively simple way, "The
> Cold Heaven" is a poem which suggests that there is an overall pur-
> pose to life; and it does so by the intrinsically poetic action of its
> rhymes, its rhythms, and its exultant intonation.[11]

With "exultant" in that last phrase Heaney puts his finger on the scale against Larkin's poem: it is the only word in the sentence that distin-guishes Yeats's achievement from Larkin's. We can't miss the opportunis-tic pressure on "positive" and "commitments." It would be implausible to argue that the art of "Aubade" is inferior to that of "The Cold Heaven" or that Larkin's inventions and redirections of consciousness are less pro-ductive than Yeats's. The internal alliterations in the line "Intricate rented world begins to rouse" are as far-reaching as any detail in Yeats's poem, the rousing being felt as spuriously energetic. What makes the difference to Heaney is that Larkin's poetic inventiveness is put to the service of a bad attitude that disavows exultation, while Yeats's serves a cause that has the grandeur of epic and tragic daring.

Heaney's account of the two poems is unfair. "The Cold Heaven," he says, is an "extraordinary visionary exclamation." The heaven it intuits is "an image of superabundant life," whereas Larkin sees nothing when he lifts his eyes but "a great absence." In Larkin, the negative evidence "demoralizes the affirmative impulse." Yeats's attitude is the "fortitude and defiance manifested in tragic art." "The Cold Heaven," like Yeats's "Man and the Echo," is "far more vital and undaunted" than "Aubade." Larkin is negative, Yeats positive. Larkin allows himself to be defeated by material conditions, Yeats like the tragic hero laughs into the face of death, as in "Lapis Lazuli," "Gaiety transfiguring all that dread." But Heaney doesn't acknowledge that much of Yeats's poem is post-Nietzschean rant.

Near the end of the lecture Heaney turns the comparison of Yeats and Larkin, in these two poems, into a rhetoric of poetry:

> in order that human beings bring about the most radiant conditions for themselves to inhabit, it is essential that the vision of reality which poetry offers should be transformative, more than just a print-out of the given circumstances of its time and place. . . . The truly creative writer, by interposing his or her perception and expression, will transfigure the conditions and effect thereby what I have been calling 'the redress of poetry.' The world is different after it has been read by a Shakespeare or an Emily Dickinson or a Samuel Beckett because it has been augmented by their reading of it. Indeed, Beckett is a very clear example of a writer who is Larkin's equal in not flinching from the ultimate bleakness of things, but who then goes on to do something positive with the bleakness. For it is not the apparent pessimism of Beckett's world-view that constitutes his poetic genius: his excellence resides in his working out a routine in the playhouse of his art which is both true to the depressing goings-on in the house of actuality and—more important—a transformation of them. It is because of his transformative way with language, his mixture of word-play and merciless humour, that Beckett the writer has life and has it more abundantly than the conditions endured by Beckett the citizen might seem to warrant.

At that point, Heaney is ready to present a theory of poetry which he evidently thinks should gain universal approval:

> We go to poetry, we go to literature in general, to be forwarded within ourselves. . . . What is at work in this most original and illuminating poetry is the mind's capacity to conceive a new plane of regard for itself, a new scope for its own activity."[12]

Offered a choice between a poem that is allegedly negative and defeatist and one that is exultant, uplifting, and fortifying, who would hesitate? And yet the argument is as seriously askew as Milosz's: it amounts, as Milosz's does, to telling a poet what he must say, what he must do, what attitude to life and death he will take, what intonations he will avoid, which of his moods he will turn into a conviction. This is clear in Heaney's emphasis upon the words "positive," "transfigure," and "transformative." The effect of the Latinate words, reiterated with such insistence, is to squash the debate. In the claim that Beckett rather than Larkin has life and has it more abundantly, Heaney's recourse to the cliché aims at protecting "life" from scrutiny or from any attempt to ask what this appeal to "life" enjoins. Heaney is not willing to argue a case; he reposes on his insistence that the value of a poem is directly proportionate to its determination to fortify its readers. If we go a further mile or two down that road we'll meet Richard Rorty telling us to sponsor "a religion of literature, in which works of the secular imagination replace Scripture as the principal source of inspiration and hope for each new generation."[13]

Heaney and Milosz are emotivists, according to MacIntyre's definition: they assert their merely personal preferences while trying to present them as objective and impersonal. They have no criteria to which they may appeal. In default of such criteria, they resort to merely assertive gestures, employing words with which debate on the relevant issues is futile. "Life" as they use the word is a mere counter, designed to fend off every call for clarification. Supposedly we know what it means and concur in the implied claim that no specification of its kinds is required. There is no sense of the difference between one life and another, or of the contradictions operative within any one life. Indeed, Larkin's "Aubade" should be cited again to make the point that in an implied scene of life and death it avoids the slogans that Milosz and Heaney so easily resort to. "Aubade" imagines the middle passage, doing without slogans while doing the best it can.

I V

Not that I am willing to give up the word "life" merely because it is vulnerable to such appropriations as Milosz's and Heaney's. "Life" *is* a necessary word, as Leavis felt impelled to claim in the introductory chapter of *Nor Shall My Sword*. Indeed, Leavis is the critic to go to when it is a question of making available to literary criticism a concept as portentous as that of "life." He did not avoid the word, but he rarely used it as if it had axiomatic force or as if, to achieve decisive victory in an argument, he had only to bring it forward, the biggest gun. I concede—indeed it is his most serious defect as a critic—that he often made a large claim for one writer by depreciating another: to exalt Lawrence he thought he had to reduce Eliot. And on those occasions he indulged himself in rhetorical devices no better than Milosz's and Heaney's. At one point, to enforce Lawrence's advantage as a critic over Eliot, Leavis said that "his genius manifests itself in a sure sense of the difference between what makes *for* life and what makes against it."[14] That is woefully boisterous, but Leavis was convinced that he had already, in several books and essays, produced sufficient evidence and particularity to justify the rhetorical flourish. Especially in his later essays he claimed that he was entitled to speak the word "life"—as a supreme value and to sustain a large claim—because he had already clarified his sense of it in critical work on Shakespeare, Wordsworth, Blake, Dickens, Lawrence, and Tolstoy. Immediately after the sentence about Lawrence that I've quoted, Leavis acknowledged the rhetorical temptation and claimed that he had sufficiently adverted to it:

> But 'life' is a large word. What *is* life? To try and define it would be futile. The advantage the critic enjoys when justifying *his* use of it and of his other indispensable terms is that he has the work of a creative writer in front of him; he is preoccupied with referring as

sensitively, faithfully and closely to *that* as he is able. The terms are prompted by the created thing, and he in turn gives them, for the reader, their charge of special meaning, their due specific force, by means, essentially, of a tact of particular reference to the given work as present—that is the aim—in the evoked experience of it (a critical process that is, in its wholly subservient and instrumental way, creative).[15]

Leavis is claiming an advantage for the literary critic over the philosopher, who apparently has no great creative work in front of him to which he is subordinate. As a result, the philosopher is at greater risk of using "life" and other large words as if they had axiomatic value or the force of his own authority.

But Leavis is alert to the danger of emotivism. "It should be possible to go beyond mere assertion," he says.[16] The going beyond is made possible, he claims, by two considerations. The first is the collaborative nature of literary criticism as he practices it:

What, of its nature, the critical activity aims at, in fact, is an exchange, a collaborative exchange, a corrective and creative interplay of judgments. For though my judgment asks to be confirmed and appeals for concurrence in a recognition that the thing is *so*, the response I expect at best will be of the form, 'Yes, but—', the 'but' standing for qualifications, corrections, shifts of emphasis, refinements, additions.[17]

Again, to make a contrast, Leavis has philosophers in mind and especially, I think, his Cambridge colleague and friend Wittgenstein, who never allowed his classroom thinking to be impeded by a raised interrogative hand.

The second consideration is more questionable. In reading a short poem with a class, "one moves judiciously," Leavis maintains, "from critical judgment to critical judgment and makes a comment the justice of which no one would think of disputing." When one has arrived at the final comment, "there is hardly any need for the critical summing-up; the case is made."[18] Perhaps it is; but seven critical judgments are not necessarily more convincing than any one of them. At the same time, Leavis's procedure is far superior, far stronger evidence of "life" in the critic, than Milosz's or Heaney's, which assumes that the crucial terms of judgment and value, including especially "life," are already there, complete in their certitude, to be simply called upon.

But I should give a clearer account of Leavis's dealings with "life," its entailments, the word and its vibrations, in his responsiveness to different forms of it. I have in view his reading of Wordsworth's first great poem, "The Ruined Cottage." The poem tells a story of passive suffering, the devastation of a life; how Margaret sinks into the relentlessness of her circumstances. Her husband Robert enlists in the army and is never heard of again, she loses her two children, and dies, leaving nothing but a ruined cottage. The story is told to the poet by a pedlar, whom the poem calls the Wanderer. Poet and Wanderer respond to the catastrophe differently, but the difference is not gross: we are not faced with anything as blunt as a moral contrast. But gradually it emerges that the Poet is susceptible to particular evidences of suffering without any of the protections that the Wanderer has taken to himself. Over the years, the Wanderer has become skilled in consolations, or at least in Stoic acceptances. He no longer feeds on disquiet, or disturbs "The calm of nature with our restless thoughts."[19] He has found it possible to resolve the most extreme human afflictions by appeal to the continuing life of the natural world—what Milosz calls "life everlasting" and "life eternal." In *The Tempest* Miranda says to her father, while the storm is still raging, "O, I have suffered / With those that I saw suffer." (I.ii.5–6) Wordsworth says of the Wanderer: "He could *afford* to suffer / With those whom he saw suffer." (lines 370–371) That is the severest thing said of him, but it stays in the mind through the more ranging sentiments when the Wanderer reflects on Margaret, now dead:

> She sleeps in the calm earth, and peace is here.
> I well remember that those very plumes,
> Those weeds, and the high spear-grass on that wall,
> By mist and silent rain-drops silvered o'er,
> As once I passed, into my heart conveyed
> So still an image of tranquillity,

> So calm and still, and looked so beautiful
> Amid the uneasy thoughts which filled my mind,
> That what we feel of sorrow and despair
> From ruin and from change, and all the grief
> That passing shows of Being leave behind,
> Appeared an idle dream, that could maintain,
> Nowhere, dominion o'er the enlightened spirit
> Whose meditative sympathies repose
> Upon the breast of Faith. I turned away,
> And walked along my road in happiness. (941–956)

That word "repose," coming with the emphasis of its being placed at the end of the verse line before sinking "upon the breast of Faith," is as telling as the complacency with which "the passing shows of Being"—these including Margaret's sufferings and death—are left behind.

Leavis makes the point that Poet and Wanderer are both Wordsworth:

> The 'I' is the actual Wordsworth . . . for whom the thought of the poor woman's suffering is not a matter of 'emotion recollected in tranquillity.' The Wanderer is the ideal Wordsworth he aspires, in an effort of imaginative realization, to be. So little can the actual Wordsworth achieve such assured tranquillity that he is tormented by a compulsion that makes him expose himself to the contemplating he can hardly endure.[20]

Leavis doesn't mention that at one point, during an interval in the telling of the story, the Poet tries to acquire something of the Wanderer's calm of mind by resolving the dead Margaret's suffering not in the greater good of everlasting life but in the "secret spirit of humanity":

> I stood, and leaning o'er the garden wall
> Reviewed that Woman's sufferings; and it seemed
> To comfort me while with a brother's love
> I blessed her in the impotence of grief.

> Then towards the cottage I returned; and traced
> Fondly, though with an interest more mild,
> That secret spirit of humanity
> Which, 'mid the calm oblivious tendencies
> Of nature, 'mid her plants, and weeds, and flowers,
> And silent overgrowings, still survived. (921–930)

Reference to the secret spirit of humanity is as far as the Poet's explicitness can go. It isn't far, and within a few lines it is virtually set aside by the more comprehensive assurance of the Wanderer which I've already quoted.

But I have given enough detail to show that Leavis's recourse to the vocabulary of "life," unequivocal as it is, is justified by his sense of particular lives, their differences and similarities. It is because his feeling for individual lives is so acute that he can invoke without apology the general term in ways that Milosz's unquestioning invocations, and Heaney's, can't achieve.

V

At the end of *After Virtue* MacIntyre gives his conclusion and claims that it is very clear:

> It is that on the one hand we still, in spite of the efforts of three centuries of moral philosophy and one of sociology, lack any coherent rationally defensible statement of a liberal individualist point of view; and that, on the other hand, the Aristotelian tradition can be restated in a way that restores intelligibility and rationality to our moral and social attitudes and commitments.[21]

I am not competent to judge whether the case for the Aristotelian tradition has been made. The question I ask is different. MacIntyre deplores what he regards as the chaos of our moral discourse, and he offers Aristotle's account of the virtues as the only rationally coherent system we might still resort to. But are we quite sure that a system of rationality and knowledge and virtue is what we want? It seems to me that MacIntyre places too much reliance on knowing. He doesn't take account of Empson's admonition, in *Seven Types of Ambiguity*, that "the object of life, after all, is not to understand things, but to maintain one's defences and equilibrium and live as well as one can; it is not only maiden aunts who are placed like this."[22] Empson also claims that people tend to make up their minds, in practical questions of human relations, much more in terms of certain vague rich intimate words—such words as "honest" and "fool"—than in terms of the clear words of their official language. He also claims that the formulae of a religion, such as Christianity or Buddhism, are interpreted in many ways, some exalted, some merely civilizing, some definitely harmful, "and that when actively at work in a society they form a kind of shrubbery of smaller ideas, which may be the most important part of their influence, yet which also may be a half-conscious protest against the formulae, a means of keeping them at bay."[23] MacIntyre might retort that Empson's affection for these informalities and subversions is precisely what is wrong with the current moral discourse. I must not put words into his mouth, but I wonder what people would do with a system of moral reference if MacIntyre were to give them such a thing. I sympathize with his frustration in not being able to judge between John Rawls's theory of justice and Robert Nozick's. Rawls's is based on need, Nozick's on entitlement. Their terms are incommensurate: it is impossible to bring them into the same field of debate. If you accept one theory rather than the other, your choice is arbitrary. But it seems to me that an articulate system, precisely because it is a system, is likely to deploy its terms as slogans. When Rawls speaks of need, and Nozick of entitlement, each of these terms acquires an aura, a penumbra of apparently achieved warmth which tends to disengage intelligence from the question in hand and make judgment feel ashamed of itself. That is the work of a slogan, as we've seen in Milosz and Heaney. The slogans are exclusive, designed to keep out rival claimants. They become technical terms, around each of which there is a *cordon sanitaire*. This doesn't apply to Empson's complex words, like "fool" and "honest." These words don't lend themselves, as Rawls's "need" and Nozick's "entitlement" do, to technical exclusiveness:

they have been in the language and therefore in the rough-and-tumble of the culture for so long that they are saturated with different connotations. When you use one of these Empsonian words, you try to point up the meaning or the range of meanings you need, but you are aware of the other irregular meanings pressing for recognition. A different problem arises with "life." To be fair in the use of the word, you have to submit its sloganeering pretensions to the evidence of actual or imagined lives, however contradictory these may be. The history of philosophy and of literary criticism has shown that apparently innocent words tend to become ideologically charged, as if they wanted to turn themselves into manifestos or institutions: structure becomes Structuralism, form Formalism, existence Existentialism, phenomenon Phenomenology, pragmatic Pragmatism, and in each case disinterestedness gives way to a note of institutional arrogance. The only hope seems to me to remain in efforts of particularity, analysis, and irony. These efforts will not release us from the murky air of rhetoric, but there is no escaping that. Each of us wants to win.

V I

MacIntyre appeals to "the Aristotelian tradition" in moral philosophy. Can any tradition be appealed to in literary criticism? At the University of Chicago many years ago a group of scholar-critics (R.S. Crane, Elder Olson, and R. P. McKeon among them) claimed the Aristotelian tradition for themselves, and offered formidable readings in that light, but they did not win many hearts. At present, no school of criticism holds power, except among its scholars. I can speak only of what I think should be the case, just as MacIntyre thinks that Aristotle should be the case. A school of criticism would be concerned with Poetics; that is, with principles of language and form operative in works of literature. Locally, it would be concerned with methods of reading: how to read a poem, a work of fiction, a page. And it should act upon a number of related assumptions. Put with necessary brevity: it should ponder the relations among certain critical positions which I designate as Susanne K. Langer,

Louise M. Rosenblatt, D. W. Harding, Geoffrey Hill, and Kenneth Burke. Langer, for her emphasis on the virtuality of art and literature, that they exist to be perceived and not otherwise to be appropriated. Rosenblatt, for her exposition of "aesthetic reading," reading that constitutes a lived-through experience rather than the mere reception of a message. D. W. Harding, for his argument, in *Experience into Words*, that writers are distinguished from other people by their capacity to bring language—the detail and quality of the language in which they write—to bear upon their thinking at the earliest stage of it and all the way thereafter: they think only in language and subject to its possibilities. Hill, for his emphasis on the antiphonal character of a writer's language, in literature and criticism; how it acknowledges the recalcitrance of the objective world and the recalcitrance, no less, of the language in which he or she works; and how a scruple in a writer takes the form of resistance to her own impulses, such that her language "turns upon itself" and interrogates itself.[24] Kenneth Burke, for his rhetoric, his sense of form and style as responsive to human desires and fulfilments. I have written of these exemplars in several books. There is no merit in going over the same ground again.

THE DEATH OF SATAN

"Hell itself, although eternal, dates from the revolt of Lucifer."
—Samuel Beckett, *The Unnamable*

IN J. F. POWERS'S STORY "PRINCE OF DARKNESS," THE ARCHBISHOP, who has decided to send Father Burner to yet another nondescript curacy rather than promote him to parish priest, complains to him:

> Today there are few saints, fewer sinners, and everybody is already saved. We are all heroes in search of an underdog. As for villains, the classic kind with no illusions about themselves, they are . . . extinct. The very devil, for instance—where the devil is the devil today, Father?[1]

But wherever the devil is lurking, we have to feel his force. In one of the prefaces to the New York edition of his fictions, Henry James recalled his dealings with "The Turn of the Screw." He regarded his Peter Quint and Miss Jessel not as ghosts, but as "goblins, elves, imps, demons as loosely constructed as those of the old trials for witchcraft." The problem James faced was how to convey the depths of the sinister without having each example of it—"the limited deplorable presentable instance"—drop far short of the telling comprehensiveness. He thought he had solved the problem by having his reader do most of the work:

Only make the reader's general vision of evil intense enough, I said to myself—and that already is a charming job—and his own experience, his own imagination, his own sympathy (with the children) and horror (of their false friends) will supply him quite sufficiently with all the particulars. Make him *think* the evil, make him think it for himself, and you are released from weak specifications.[2]

A page or two later, James glances at the moral question his procedure entailed. Readers of "The Turn of the Screw" often accused him of committing a monstrous emphasis. He answered that he had done no such thing, his values were "positively all blanks save as far as an excited horror, a promoted pity, a created expertness" in the reader proceeded to read into them "more or less fantastic figures":

Of high interest to the author meanwhile—and by the same stroke a theme for the moralist—the artless resentful reaction of the entertained person who has abounded in the sense of the situation. He visits his abundance, morally, on the artist—who has but clung to an ideal of faultlessness.[3]

I have brought forward those moments in Powers and James because between them they cover most of the ground of what I want to say. They raise the main issues: thinking the evil, weak and strong specifications of it, the propensity of readers who, given an inch, take an ell, and readers who find their vague sense of a mythical evil figure affronted by an author's rival specifications of him. At the end of Powers's story the Archbishop, in a brief instruction to Father Burner, says: "I trust that in your new appointment you will find not peace but a sword."[4]

I I

In an essay, "On the Devil, and Devils," and again in the *Defence of Poetry*, Shelley says that the Devil "owes everything to Milton":

Dante and Tasso present us with a very gross idea of him: Milton divested him of a sting, hoofs, and horns; clothed him with the sublime grandeur of a graceful but tremendous spirit—and restored him to the society.[5]

He is a Devil, Shelley said, "very different from the popular personification of evil malignity and it is a mistake to suppose that he was intended for an idealism of implacable hate, cunning, and refinement of device to inflict the utmost anguish on an enemy." Milton, according to Shelley, "so far violated all that part of the popular creed which is susceptible of being preached and defended in argument, as to allege no superiority in moral virtue to his God over his Devil." He "mingled as it were the elements of human nature, as colours upon a single pallet, and arranged them into the composition of his great picture, according to the laws of epic truth; that is, according to the laws of that principle by which a series of actions of intelligent and ethical beings, developed in rhythmical language, are calculated to excite the sympathy and antipathy of succeeding generations of mankind."[6]

Those familiar sentences are worth quoting because they remind us that one of the difficulties in interpreting *Paradise Lost* arises from its several acknowledgments, hard to make consistent. Milton took the popular personification of evil into account if mainly to affront it. He recalled with more respect the allegorical tradition, from the medieval morality plays to Marlowe's *Dr. Faustus, Tamburlane*, and *The Jew of Malta*—it is the note of Satan's "Evil be thou my good" (4.110) which recalls Isaiah's "Woe unto them that call evil good, and good evil" (6.20). Milton also respected his duty to the Bible, and chose to incur a further obligation to the tradition of tragedy from Aeschylus to Shakespeare. He obeyed the laws of epic truth, as Shelley says. And to thicken the plot he undertook what Paul Ricoeur has called "the foolish business of trying to justify God."[7]

Not that Milton was of many minds when he spoke in his own behalf about evil. In a famous passage in *Areopagitica* he said that "good and evil we know in the field of this world grow up together almost inseparably," a sentence that recalls Christ's parable in Matthew's Gospel about the good seeds and the tares sown among the wheat by the farmer's enemy. The wise farmer says: "Let both grow together until the harvest, and in the time of harvest I will say to the reapers, 'Gather ye together first the tares, and bind them in bundles to burn them: but gather the wheat into my barn'" (13:30). "It was from out the rind of one apple tasted," Milton says, "that the knowledge of good and evil, as two twins cleaving together, leaped forth into the world." "Assuredly," he continues, "we bring not innocence into the world, we bring impurity much rather; that which purifies us is trial, and trial is by what is contrary."[8] In the *De Doctrina Christiana* he says that God is concerned in the production of evil in only one of two ways: "either, first, he permits its existence by throwing no impediment in the way of natural causes and free agents, . . . or, secondly, he causes evil by the infliction of judgments, which is called the evil of punishment."[9] In the same spirit Milton says that "God, who is infinitely good, cannot be the doer of wickedness, or of the evil of sin." "It is not allowable to consider him as in the smallest instance the author of sin."[10] On the contrary, "out of the wickedness of sin he produces good."[11] Of the Tree of Knowledge, Milton says that "it was called the tree of knowledge of good and evil from the event; for since Adam tasted it, we not only know evil, but we know good only by means of evil. For it is by evil that virtue is chiefly exercised, and shines with greater brightness."[12] A note in Milton's commonplace book reads:

> Why does God permit evil? So that reason can support virtue. For virtue is attested by evil, is illuminated and trained. As Lactantius says: that Reason and Judgement may have a field in which they may exercise themselves by choosing the things that are good and shunning the things that are evil. . . .[13]

But Milton lets the narrator of book 4 of *Paradise Lost* refer to "our death the Tree of Knowledge" in Eden as "Knowledge of good bought dear by knowing ill" (4.222). He reverts to the position of *Areopagitica* by having Adam in book 5 say, when Eve has told him of her dream:

> yet be not sad.
> Evil into the mind of god or man

May come and go, so unapproved, and leave
No spot or blame behind:[14]

—a thought formidably perverted by Satan when he tempts Eve in book 9:

. . . Or will God incense his ire
For such a petty trespass, and not praise
Rather your dauntless virtue, whom the pain
Of death denounced, whatever thing death be,
Deterred not from achieving what might lead
To happier life, knowledge of good and evil;
Of good, how just? Of evil, if what is evil
Be real, why not known, since easier shunned?
God therefore cannot hurt ye, and be just;
Not just, not God; not feared then, nor obeyed:
Your fear itself of death removes the fear.
Why then was this forbid? Why but to awe,
Why but to keep ye low and ignorant,
His worshipers; he knows that in the day
Ye eat thereof, your eyes that seem so clear,
Yet are but dim, shall perfectly be then
Opened and cleared, and ye shall be as gods,
Knowing both good and evil as they know. (9.692–709)

What makes this compelling, and not only to Eve, is the rapidity with
which Satan moves from one set of values to another and leaps over the
anomalies among them: going from heroic values stirred in "dauntless"
and "Deterred not from achieving," to worldly intelligence appealed to in
"real," then to niceties of logic in "Not just, not God; not feared then, nor
obeyed," and rushing to the politics of class resentment in "Why then
was this forbid?" clinched by the optical metaphor, dim eyes that can be
opened and cleared, "and ye shall be as gods." He mentions obedience
only to say that if God isn't God he's in no position to demand it.

    In *Paradise Lost* Milton retains the same range of values as in *Areo-
pagitica,* but he slows the movement from one to the next. Kermode says

that "we are always being told the proper way to think about Satan."[15]
The trouble is that Milton tells us different things at different times, and
he shows us things from time to time that don't square with what we have
been told. We are repeatedly told that Satan is "th' infernal Serpent"
(1.34), he is "Hypocrisy, the only evil that walks/Invisible, except to God
alone" (3.683–684), "the Fiend" (4.393). He appeals to Necessity, "the
tyrant's plea" (4.394); in book 9 he is "the spirited sly snake" (9.613),
"the wily adder" (9.625), "the dire snake" (9.643), "the guileful Tempter"
(9.567), and "the Evil One" (9.463). But he is also shown to be, at least
in the first books, the dauntless hero who has sent Blake, Shelley, and
Harold Bloom into raptures, fantasies of self-creation. Bloom is even
ready to take seriously the piece of casuistry in book 5 where Satan claims
that he and his kind were "self-begot, self-raised/By our own quick'ning
power" (5.860–861). The decisive answer to this is Adam's in book 8:

> For man to tell how human life began
> Is hard; for who himself beginning knew? (8.250–251)

I am not unmoved by Satan as villain-hero, blood-brother to Byron's
Cain, but I deplore the strutting and remain disappointed by the critical
sublimists.

But Satan is diminished not so much by the heroics, meretricious as
they are, as by the penury of his vices. At least we can feel, watching him
in his rebellious scenes: well, this is absurd in the long view, but superb in
the short one. But when we watch him indulging himself in the petty
vices, we feel: why, he's no better than we are. The reduction of Satan to
the human scale of vice, and further to the pettiest of these, may have had
some consequence in the gradual erasure of Satan, if not his death. When
he sees Adam and Eve kissing and about to make love, we read that

> Aside the Devil turned
> For envy, yet with jealous leer malign
> Eyed them askance, and to himself thus plained.
>   "Sight hateful, sight tormenting! Thus these two
> Imparadised in one another's arms

The happier Eden, shall enjoy their fill
Of bliss on bliss, while I to hell am thrust,
Where neither joy nor love, but fierce desire,
Among our other torments not the least,
Still unfulfilled with pain of longing pines;" (4.502–511)

The fierce desire, the result of sexual deprivation, is not a mark against Satan. The whole passage is thrilling, despite the "jealous leer malign," all the way from the happier Eden to the last great line which crowds the sense of exhausting but not exhausted frustration. The feeling is buffeted between two linguistic sets of value, the first featuring the alliteration, internal rhymes, and assonances of "Still unfulfilled"—which gathers up the contrasting "enjoy their fill" four lines back—and the second one, the second half of the line which keeps the verb—"pines"—to the end, where it removes any hope that the "pains of longing" will ever be eased. But the magnificence of the passage is not enough to make us forgive the blatant self-regard that contrasts "thus these two" with "while I to hell am thrust."

In book 9 when Eve has arranged the foolish plan of dividing the gardening work with Adam, Satan comes looking for them, but especially for Eve. He sees her among the flowers—Eve herself by an exquisite analogy "the fairest unsupported flower"—and the first effect of his seeing her is that he suspends his evil intent. It is one of the richest Spenserian moments in the poem:

Her graceful innocence, her every air
Of gesture or least action overawed
His malice, and with rapine sweet bereaved
His fierceness of the fierce intent it brought:
That space the Evil One abstracted stood
From his own evil, and for the time remained
Stupidly good, of enmity disarmed,
Of guile, of hate, of envy, of revenge;
But the hot hell that always in him burns,
Though in mid-heav'n, soon ended his delight,
And tortures him now more, the more he sees

Of pleasure not for him ordained: then soon
Fierce hate he recollects, and all his thoughts
Of mischief, gratulating, thus excites. (9.459–472)

"Bereaved" anticipates the other form of death that Satan intends for Eve
and Adam. "Stupidly good" describes the kind of merit that Milton repu-
diates in the *Areopagitica*, the "fugitive and cloistered virtue unexercised
and unbreathed, that never sallies out and seeks her adversary, but slinks
out of the race. . . ."[16] "Abstracted" makes the point that for this brief
space Satan is withdrawn from himself as if to a second self, but soon
the hot hell in him makes him recall—gratulate—his first self. It is an
extraordinary intermission, but still within the range of the small virtues
and it yields yet again to a small vice.

Earlier in book 4, there is another example of Satan's penury. He has
gained entrance to Eden, but we have to wait while Milton recites two
comparisons. Satan is a prowling wolf getting ready to attack the sheep,
and he is a thief climbing through a window of a rich burgher's house:

> Thence up he flew, and on the Tree of Life,
> The middle tree and highest there that grew,
> Sat like a cormorant; yet not true life
> Thereby regained, but sat devising death
> To them who lived; nor on the virtue thought
> Of that life-giving plant, but only used
> For prospect, what well used had been the pledge
> Of immortality. (4.194–201)

The cormorant is a strange choice, a bird generally found on cliff ledges
above rivers or the sea, before it swoops down on fish for food. Sainte-
Beuve in a remarkable note refers to a little phrase from that passage. He
warns against a certain vain curiosity he finds in some modern writers
who try to pluck out the heart of every spiritual mystery. They are like
Satan, he says, in this episode, not taking the occasion to recover his life,
"but rather using the tree only to see farther on, *for prospect*."[17] Again it is
a small vice, however sharply Sainte-Beuve spoke of it and associated it
with vanity.

But while Satan's vices are mostly the small ones, Milton gives him enormous narrative and dramatic privilege. In this poem of joy and the loss of it, as Kermode says, "we see all delight through the eyes of Satan."[18] Why would the poet do such a thing, handing over authority to an unreliable witness, if not to effect what Clifford Geertz calls the "thick description" of its scenes? If Eden is beautiful in Satan's eyes, it must in truth be far more beautiful than anything we have imagined, or beautiful in more aspects. Of course Milton doesn't give Satan an entirely free hand: he makes him give himself away and, failing that, Milton intervenes with a corrective comment. But the latitude he gives Satan, where joy and pleasure are at hand, is remarkable: we are more accustomed to this narrative daring in novels than in epic poems.

III

It seems to be common opinion that in literature Satan died in *Paradise Lost*: we see him for the last time as he languishes in Hell. It is widely assumed that he didn't survive the Enlightenment. But he was revived in several French novels in the nineteenth century, and with strange insistence in Baudelaire's *Les Fleurs du mal* and the *Journaux Intimes*. Baudelaire's Satan is not Milton's, much as Baudelaire admired Milton's. It is my impression that T. S. Eliot's essay of 1930 on Baudelaire was effective for a time in brushing aside Baudelaire's Satanism and presenting him as a poet who did not practice Christianity but asserted its necessity. Eliot regarded Satanism, so far as it was not affectation, as "an attempt to get into Christianity by the back door." But the crucial consideration for him was Baudelaire's perception "that what really matters is Sin and Redemption." Baudelaire's sense of Evil was powerful and entirely free of the machinery of the Black Mass. It was a defect of his sensibility that he had "an imperfect, vague romantic conception of Good."[19] By comparison with Dante in that respect, he was, Eliot says, a bungler. But he was a great poet because he brought about a renovation in poetic language: his renovation of an attitude toward life was no less radical. Eliot's emphasis, strongly influenced by T. E. Hulme's writings on Original Sin, made a difference to the general reception of Baudelaire in English and American literature and criticism, but many readers concluded that what Eliot really tried to do was to kidnap Baudelaire for Christianity. That part of the effort has not won many adherents. Readers of Baudelaire continue to be embarrassed by his Satanism and to pass quickly over the appearances of Satan in the poems.

But that procedure may not be decisive. Jonathan Culler has been calling for a different kind of attention to Baudelaire's Satanic verses. In a recent essay he quotes Baudelaire as telling Flaubert, when Flaubert chastised him for making too much of the spirit of Evil, that "I have always been obsessed by the impossibility of accounting for certain actions or sudden thoughts of man without the hypothesis of the intervention of an evil force outside him."[20] In an essay on Theodore de Banville, Baudelaire wrote of modern art as having an essentially demonic tendency:

> And it seems that this infernal part of man, which man takes pleasure in explicating to himself, grows larger every day, as if the Devil were amusing himself by fattening it through artificial means, inspired by force-feeders, patiently stuffing humankind in his farmyards, to prepare more succulent nourishment for himself.[21]

Culler takes that passage seriously. Starting with the first poem of *Les Fleurs du mal*—"Au lecteur"—he responds to Satan's force of presence in Baudelaire's poems and offers several possible readings. The Devil is the one who pulls the strings. He weakens our will, perverts our understanding. He is our Prince of Ennui. He is also a familiar in our most dangerous acts of self-consciousness. Satan has won, Baudelaire claims, not by keeping himself heroic, but by becoming soft: his *niaiserie* has replaced brilliance and spirit.[22]

Culler emphasizes, as Baudelaire does from time to time, the impersonal character of evil. Culler says:

> To dismiss Satan as *just* a "personification" of evil, though, and thus a fiction, requires remarkable confidence about what can and what cannot act, about what forces there are at work in the universe. Behind the wish to dismiss him as personification may lie the wishful

presumption that only human individuals can act, that they control the world and that there are no other agents; but the world would be a very different place if this were true. Much of its character, its difficulty, its mystery, comes from the effects produced by actions of other sorts of agents, which our grammars may or may not personify: history, classes, capital, freedom, public opinion—forces not graspable at the level of the empirical actions of individuals but which seem to control the world and give events meaningful and often oppressive structures.[23]

It follows, in Culler's reading, that Satan in Baudelaire's poems acts in several allegorical scenes. Like Anguish, Autumn, Beauty, Ennui, Hope, Hatred, and other figures, Satan's presence in the poems raises questions about persons, about where they begin and end, and what their relations are to body, spirit, and history. It questions the axiom according to which each of us is autonomous, a self among equally autonomous selves.

I V

In the end, Culler wants to clear the air of theology and Satanism by removing Baudelaire's poems to politics. But he acknowledges that a certain violence of interpretation is entailed. Besides, the culture of his own society makes that removal difficult. The proposal to take the mystery out of religion, in America, has offered psychology, not politics, as its popular form and epistemology as its refined form. Both offers meet in Emerson, as in "Experience," where he writes:

It is very unhappy, but too late to be helped, the discovery we have made that we exist. That discovery is called the Fall of Man. Ever afterwards we suspect our instruments. We have learned that we do not see directly, but mediately, and that we have no means of correcting these colored and distorting lenses which we are, or of computing the amount of their errors.[24]

One tradition of American poetry from Emerson to John Ashbery and A. R. Ammons has been engaged with Emerson's version of the Fall of Man and with the process of suspecting our instruments of knowledge. In this tradition, evil is merely the nuisance that epistemologists have to cope with. It is not sin. It is not what the "familiar compound ghost" of "Little Gidding" tells his pupil it is—

> the rending pain of re-enactment
>> Of all that you have done, and been; the shame
>> Of motives late revealed, and the awareness
> Of things ill done and done to others' harm
>> Which once you took for exercise of virtue.[25]

In the Emersonian tradition, evil is merely a problem for knowledge. Emerson does not believe, as Levinas does, that ethics precedes ontology. In Emerson's tradition the most acute necessity is to convert the world to ourselves, or at least to stimulate the conviction that the imagination can so convert it. Otherwise we are fated to live in an alien world, impenetrable and opaque. But there is an attendant risk that the imagination will engage in this work only speciously, and that the conversion will be a fraud. Poets in league with philosophic idealism are susceptible to this temptation, which is what Yeats meant by the passage in the *Autobiographies* in which he said that Shelley and Whitman lacked "the vision of Evil." Their victories over the world came too easily because they did not acknowledge the force of Evil in all its forms. Stevens is the greatest poet in this tradition, and his "Esthétique du mal," while not his greatest poem, is a distinctively American response to Baudelaire's *Les Fleurs du mal*.

The "Esthétique" is a poem, or a sequence of poems, as Kermode says, "about the acceptance of evil in reality, and the discovery 'in this bad,' of 'The last purity of the knowledge of good.'"[26] Evil, in Stevens's poems, is external to begin with and often all the way through; it is Emerson's version of necessity, *Ananke*. In the "Esthétique du mal" it is represented by Vesuvius and the refractory way things are. It is everything that is the case, every obstacle that life and nature put up to thwart the individual imagination. Evil becomes internal only because the imagination takes over the monster and incorporates it in itself. In "The Poems of Our Climate" Stevens speaks of "the evilly compounded, vital I," but evilly compounded is not the same as bad, it has nothing to do with evil, it means the self that has acknowledged the refractoriness of the world and taken to itself a correspondingly sturdy sense of life. Evil is not an ethical constituent of the self, it never incurs the risk of damnation, it merely gives the imagination more work to do. But the more work the imagination has to do, the better. So this poem speaks of paradise well lost, since it holds out the possibility of creating a new paradise, a song of the earth in worldly speech.

I will not go through the whole sequence, or even make notes in the margin. I will merely offer a few sentences, more or less ad lib, on its major themes. The first sections of the "Esthétique" reflect on pain, how it separates the speaker from his otherwise freely imagined world. "After great pain a formal feeling comes," Emily Dickinson writes, and the formality is residual, it testifies to where the life has been. In Stevens's poem, pain comes in various forms: as *malheur*, the sob beyond invention, the soldier's wound, life as a bitter aspic. There is always a supremacy above pain, as here the sky, the moon, and night, but Stevens finds consolation—the good issuing from evil—everywhere:

> It is pain that is indifferent to the sky
> In spite of the yellow of the acacias, the scent
> Of them in the air still hanging heavily
> In the hoary-hanging night. It does not regard
> This freedom, this supremacy, and in
> Its own hallucination never sees
> How that which rejects it saves it in the end.[27]

Hallucinations in Stevens's poetry are saving things. Here they postpone the recognition that the immediate obstacle, the sky, is redemptive in the end because it retains the value of the pain when the pain has lapsed. The sky does not hold out forever against the imagination. But meanwhile there are hard moments in which the will demands that what the speaker thinks be true. It is a severe demand, rarely acknowledged in Stevens, and the speaker is so exasperated that he imagines a third world without knowledge—it is third because the first is the given world and the second is the world we try to make while thinking of it as the work of knowing:

> This creates a third world without knowledge,
> In which no one peers, in which the will makes no
> Demands. It accepts whatever is as true,
> Including pain, which, otherwise, is false.
> In the third world, then, there is no pain. Yes, but
> What lover has one in such rocks, what woman,
> However known, at the centre of the heart? (323)

That is as if to say: All you can do in the third world is accept for truth reality as given. The will, being free of knowledge, or of the desire to know, is withdrawn, passive. Pain is accepted like everything else because it is true. If it were not accepted, it would be false, a scandal to the values of the third world, such as they are. In this third world there is no pain because the mind doesn't differentiate any experience as pain. It is like Utopia. Yes, but who would want to be relieved of desire, love, passion, pain, dread?

In the third section of "Esthétique", Stevens alludes without naming them to Dante, Milton, Adam, and Christ, and seems to say that now that heaven, hell, and earth are one and the same, we could have managed quite well without Christ, the "over-human god." He has weakened us by his pity. The world as it is would be sufficient without him:

> As if hell, so modified, had disappeared,
> As if pain, no longer satanic mimicry,
> Could be borne, as if we were sure to find our way. (316)

I take satanic mimicry to be the evil in the world, introjected as pain. We could bear it, "the honey of common summer" being sufficient alleviation.

Part of the fourth section has been subject to many different readings:

> The genius of misfortune
> Is not a sentimentalist. He is
> That evil, that evil in the self, from which
> In desperate hallow, rugged gesture, fault
> Falls out on everything: the genius of
> The mind, which is our being, wrong and wrong,
> The genius of the body, which is our world,
> Spent in the false engagements of the mind. (316–317)

Even here, evil is not Satan's work, it is whatever incites one's sense of evil and keeps it active, such that in a beautiful falling "fault/Falls out on everything." It makes the genius of the mind think of itself, mistakenly, as separate from the body, and makes the genius of the body think of itself as separate from the mind, such that its necessary engagements with the mind are false. Like Milton, Stevens refuses to think of body and mind as separate. Both would agree with Raphael, who speaks to Adam of things "Each in their several active spheres assigned,/Till body up to spirit work, in bounds/Proportioned to each kind" (5.477–479). The movement is analogical, not disjunctive.

The eighth section of the "Esthétique" begins:

> The death of Satan was a tragedy
> For the imagination. A capital
> Negation destroyed him in his tenement
> And, with him, many blue phenomena.

That is: the death of Satan was a tragedy because the imagination had less work to do and it lost the strong specifications of reality as incitement to its proper activity. It lost many blue phenomena, blue because in Stevens that is the imagination's color. Satan's death entails a loss of sensibility, or of part of one's sensibility: it turns us into logical positivists, bereft of incantation. The death of Satan, according to this poem, has left phantoms displaced. These are the spirits that Stevens in "Sunday Morning" at once acknowledged and denied: there is no longer, he says, a "golden underground" or "isle/Melodious, where spirits gat them home."

This isle is as defunct as the diction that once respected the spirits. So again in the "Esthétique du mal," which in many aspects is a revision, bewildered indeed, of "Sunday Morning." Stevens does what he can with the hard issues—necessity, limitation, pain, war, death—but he can't think of any way to end his poem except by reverting to "the right chorale," the humanist paradise of being alive. Still, he acknowledges a scruple:

> One might have thought of sight, but who could think
> Of what it sees, for all the ill it sees?
> Speech found the ear, for all the evil sound,
> But the dark italics it could not propound.
> And out of what one sees and hears and out
> Of what one feels, who could have thought to make
> So many selves, so many sensuous worlds,
> As if the air, the mid-day air, was swarming
> With the metaphysical changes that occur,
> Merely in living as and where we live. (326)

This is companionable with "Sunday Morning" except for the rhyming couplet inserted between lines otherwise continuous. Usually in Stevens, it is enough that speech finds the ear. In "The Course of a Particular" the "final finding of the ear" is close to the disclosure of "the thing/Itself."[28] But here:

> Speech found the ear, for all the evil sound,
> But the dark italics it could not propound.

It is as decisive as a couplet from Pope's *Dunciad*. Italics occur in another medium, print rather than speech. I assume that the dark italics are those forces or presences in reality that the imagination can't propound. They must be evil, according to Stevens's sense of evil. To propound is to bring forward for consideration, but speech can't do this because the imagination can't foresee the forms the evil will take. The lines are Stevens's most generous concession, that there are forces of evil, forms of unpre-

dictable necessity and opacity, that the humanist imagination can't antici-
pate. For such an Emersonian, such a Nietzschean, it is a remarkable con-
cession. No wonder it is given in a self-enclosed rhyming couplet, and
once it has been given, the blank verse exaltation is resumed.

V

A few years ago Andrew Delbanco's book received from Stevens's
poem its title and some of its themes. Delbanco's *The Death of Satan*
argues that till about three hundred years ago evil was understood in
American culture in relation to the Fall, Adam and Eve, the Devil, and
original sin, but that by 1700 this understanding had waned. The main
causes of the waning were the apparent success of science in explaining at
least those aspects of the natural world that needed to be explained; and
the promise of science that it would someday not only understand the
natural world but control it. One consequence of this success and that
promise was a loss of belief in essences: you might think someone a bad
person, but you didn't feel any need to detach his badness from him and
consider it in its essence. Correspondingly, Delbanco says, "belief in
embodied spirits was reduced to a superstition."[29] Ghosts were no longer
believed in; they were internalized as hallucinatory figments. It followed
that there was a weakening of the sense of sin. Certain impulses, tradition-
ally thought to be vicious, were promoted as virtues: pride, for instance,
"was rehabilitated as a defensible emotion." The Devil was domesticated
while being held at a distance: he became a foreigner, a black man, or a
cripple. Evil itself was naturalized, it lost its mystery and was identified
with deficiency, misfortune, disadvantage. In Stevens's terms, the phan-
toms were excluded from society. Delbanco might have added further
considerations. Milbank has pointed out that "from the late seventeenth
century onwards, the word 'God' came to denote merely an ultimate
causal hypothesis, rather than the eminent origin and pre-containment
of all created perfection." A first cause conceived on the model of efficient
causality, or the instantiation of logical possibility (as in Leibniz), "was
not, like the medieval God, good by definition." His goodness "had to be

'demonstrated' in terms of the necessity of local imperfections for the most perfect harmony of the whole."

In the Middle Ages, by contrast, "although there were indeed many intimations of such an approach, there was not, on the whole, any dominantly recognized 'problem of evil.'" Citing Kenneth Surin's *Theology and the Problem of Evil*, Milbank notes that "suffering and evil were not defined in such a way as to make them a theoretical problem":

> On the contrary, they were regarded as negative or predatory in relation to Being and therefore as a problem only 'solvable' in practice. Where evil was seen as the manifest upshot of a perverse will (it being presumed that without free assent there could be no perfect goodness in creatures) and suffering as the sign of the deep-seated effect of such perversity, there *was* no real problem of evil, and so no science of 'theodicy.' In the seventeenth century, by contrast, attributions of evil to the effects of the fall of demonic powers and of humanity went into decline, and thus evil was approximated to the theoretically observable fact of imperfection, to be rationally accounted for.[30]

It is not surprising, therefore, that it has become socially unacceptable to think that there is such a thing as radical evil, what Kant called "radical innate evil in human nature," a disposition, as he said, "to adopt evil *as evil* into our maxim as our incentive."[31] It is true, as Ricoeur says, that Kant "understands the Fall, free and fated of man, as the painful road of all ethical life that is of an adult character and on an adult level."[32] But even this version of the *felix culpa* is socially scandalous. We are not encouraged to see Iago as Coleridge saw him, a motiveless malignity.

But Delbanco is merely describing our *Zeitgeist*. Not to believe in the Devil is a prejudice of the *Zeitgeist*: it is not a prohibition in any particular case. It is not at all foolish to believe in the Devil, as Gide did, for instance. In *The Counterfeiters* he sees the Devil migrating from one character to another, making each of them a counterfeiter: Edouard, Pauline, Vincent, Olivier, Passavant, Bernard. In Edouard, the Devil takes the form of sophistry, novelty, fresh starts that are always false, experiments on the lives of others:

To what sophisms does he lend an ear? They must be the promptings of the devil, for if they came from anyone else, he would not listen to them. (*A quels sophismes prête-t-il l'oreille? Le diable assurement les lui souffle, car il ne les écouterait pas, venus s'autrui.*)[33]

In Lady Griffith and Vincent the Devil is boredom, even of the flesh. In Pauline, it is a need for affection so compulsive that for its satisfaction she is willing to see the lives of those dearest to her destroyed. And so for the others: in each case a fresh start is the sign that the Devil has arrived. We are not to laugh at the old music-teacher Antoine de La Perouse when near the end he says to Edouard:

Have you noticed that in this world God always keeps silent? It's only the devil who speaks. Or at least, at least . . . however carefully we listen, it's only the devil we can succeed in hearing. . . . I have often thought that the word of God was the whole of creation. But the devil seized hold of it. His noise drowns the voice of God. (*Avez-vous remarqué que, dans ce monde, Dieu se tait toujours? Il n'y a que le diable qui parle. Ou du moins, ou du moins . . . quelle que soit notre attention, ce n'est jamais que le diable que nous parvenons à entendre. . . . J'ai souvent pensé que la parole de Dieu, c'était la création tout entière. Mais le diable s'en est emparé. Son bruit couvre à present la voix de Dieu.*)[34]

More demently after a few moments, La Perouse bursts out:

No, no! . . . The devil and the Good God are one and the same; they work together. We try to believe that everything bad on earth comes from the devil, but it's because, if we didn't, we should never find strength to forgive God. (*Non! Non! . . . le diable et le Bon Dieu ne font qu'un; ils s'entendent. Nous nous efforcons de croire que tout ce qu'il a de mauvais sur la terre vient du diable; mais c'est parce qu'autrement nous ne trouverions pas en nous la force de pardonner à Dieu.*)[35]

Unintimidated by any charge of anachronism, Gide takes the Devil seriously as the force of fraud, as plausible as he is nameless and traveling incognito. Gide, as Blackmur says, "is the French puritan who nurses the devil within him, not as a poor relation as in Mann and Dostoevsky, but in his older and prouder role as the Prince of Darkness in whose service we must perform most of our acts, since he is our feudal self."[36] This last phrase, "our feudal self," reminds us that, even if we wanted to for reasons of prudence, we can't capitulate to the *Zeitgeist:* we do not coincide with ourselves at every point, we are not contemporaneous with all our impulses. Still, we are not free of the devil. The devil, as Blackmur says, exists until he is recognized; which explains why, recognizing him, we want to give him a name and then an explanation. He is most fully the Devil before he is recognized, named, or explained. I think of Neil LaButte's film *In the Company of Men*, in which two executives in a business firm are transferred out of town for six weeks. One of them, Chad, persuades the other, Howard, to find a vulnerable young woman and wound her. "Let's hurt someone," Chad says. He pretends to hate women: "I don't trust anyone who bleeds for a week and doesn't die." They meet a deaf girl in the office, and each of them tries to make her fall in love with him. Chad is successful, but Howard falls in love with her. She falls for Chad, who abandons her. When it's all over, Howard asks Chad why he ever thought of hurting someone: "Because I could," Chad answers. LaButte assumes that deliberate cruelty, person to person, is still known to be evil, though rarely called Satan.

Generally, our culture urges us to suppose that there is an empirical explanation for everything. If we knew enough about the early years of Myra Hindley, Charles Manson, Jeffrey Dahmer, and Ian Brady, we could explain what it was in the social context that impelled them to do the things they did. Nature or nurture is to blame, we would say. We would restore their deeds to the heterogeneity of society, even if we decided for our own security to keep these people in jail. "Because the society you have internalized is guilty, you are innocent": this, as Alain Finkielkraut says, sums up the credo of modern humanism."[37] But it is possible to mock this complacency, as P. C. Vey did in a recent *New Yorker* cartoon. Two men, identically morose, are walking along together. One says to the other: "With me it's neither nature nor nurture. It's Satan."[38] What is funny in the cartoon is its recourse to such an outmoded explanation. What is telling in it is the need to have recourse to such a device. No one wants to let any event transcend its explanation. Wallace Shawn has argued that "the difference between a perfectly decent person and a monster is just a few thoughts." The perfectly decent person "who follows a certain chain of reasoning, ever so slightly and subtly incorrect, becomes a perfect monster at the end of the chain." Within each thought, "other thoughts are hidden, waiting to crawl out."[39] I think it more likely that images, rather than thoughts, are the immediate occasions of evil. There is also the problem that evil people are not fully accounted for by their evil: they have other attributes, enthusiasms, ennui. "Men are accomplices to that which leaves them indifferent," as George Steiner has noted.[40] Hannah Arendt annoyed many Jews by speaking of the banality of evil and refusing to present Eichmann as a demon, evil brother to his even worse brother Hitler. She would not concede to him the chic of evil that characterizes Richard III or Iago. She insisted on mundane causes, explanations, the empirical origins of totalitarianism, even though she acknowledged herself defeated by the Holocaust. If she could, she would not let the experience of evil go beyond the reach of a historian's syntax. It is implausible that she thought her formulae adequate: the question is why she consigned her bewilderment to formulae at all. Perhaps she was thinking of "the bureaucratization of the imaginative"—Kenneth Burke's phrase—the process by which an imaginative possibility, Utopian or abysmal as it may be, is reduced to a social dimension. "There is a kind of political imagination," Robert Boyers has observed, "that can operate only by assuming that all human affairs fall under the heading of business as usual."[41]

VI

Jean Baudrillard has reinterpreted these considerations. In *The Transparency of Evil* he argues that we can no longer speak Evil or, presumably, think Evil, such is our obsession with Good. By Good he evidently means not the virtuous life or the life of a saint but the life that American TV, Wall Street, and the White House conspire to present as supremely good: bourgeois liberalism, consumer-style. We have been brainwashed to accept that image of the good life. As a result, Evil has metamorphosed into all the terroristic forms that obsess us.[42] By hunting down "the accursed share" [*la part maudite*] and allowing only positive values free rein, we have made ourselves vulnerable to the least viral attack, represented in the rhetoric of the White House as international terrorism, "weapons of mass destruction," weapons that we have but that we don't want anyone else to have. We denounce as evil every irruption of apparently archaic motives into the ensolacings of modernity. Khomeini's *fatwa* on Rushdie's *Satanic Verses* is a signal case in point.

Baudrillard thinks that Evil is no longer a moral principle: it has been translated into political terms. It has become a principle of instability and vertigo, of complexity and foreignness, of seduction, incompatibility, antagonism, and irreducibility. Since the closing of Eden, Evil has taken up residence in knowledge, where it works to analyze and separate forces that need not be separated. The consensus that Baudrillard attacks is the illusion that Good can be separated from Evil. The Good consists, he believes, in a dialectic of Good and Evil. He agrees with Milton. Evil, in practice, consists in the negation of this dialectic and, by extension, in setting up the autonomy of each, Good and Evil. Evil then founds itself on pure incompatibility, and becomes master of the game, destroying the illusion of consensus. The more things seem to join in universal comprehension and consensus, Baudrillard says, the more unavoidable the insistent images of irreducibility become. Islam will never become Western.

The answer to these quandaries is not, Baudrillard argues, the current pleasantries that feature the rhetoric of difference: pluralism and multiculturalism. Otherness differs from difference. Difference is only a nuance of the Same. "The other must be maintained in his foreignness."[43] Baudrillard refers approvingly to Roland Barthes and his book on Japan.

But we still have to "think the evil," or at least think the compounded good-and-evil. There is nothing to prevent our doing so, using religious terms or terms from religious myths. These have not been disabled. There is no reason to capitulate to what we are told is the *Zeitgeist*, secular through and through. I recall F. R. Leavis referring to "the darkness of enlightened men." If we seek a secular form of understanding, the most fruitful one still seems to me that of tragedy. I know that it is possible to repudiate tragedy, as Walter Benjamin did, and to accuse tragic thought of proposing to transcend the instances of evil and suffering. Benjamin resented the implication, in classical and Shakespearean tragedy, that evil is not the entire "story of the night" and that an evil time may somehow be redeemed. He suspected that tragic form was an attempt to lead the mind beyond evil appearances toward a principle of value and order. Benjamin rejected the consolation prize, and pointed instead to the German *Trauerspiel* which leaves temporal experience entirely unredeemed.[44] It is as if he resented the development of feeling and conviction, in Shakespeare, from *King Lear* to *A Winter's Tale*. Benjamin will have no Recognition Scenes, no promise of redemption. I see no reason to obey his injunctions. We are justified in feeling, at the end of *King Lear*, that there are operative values which may not be entirely defeated by evil otherwise regnant. Think of the Recognition Scene between Lear and Cordelia, and the image of Lear holding Cordelia in his arms while Kent says: "Is this the promis'd end?" and Edgar answers: "Or image of that horror?"[45] In our tradition, it is tragedy that restores the Devil to our society, while it presents the possibility of moving beyond his specifications, strong as they are. So we have not only *King Lear* but *Crime and Punishment*, "Heart of Darkness," *Survival in Auschwitz*, *The Periodic Table*, Celan's "Todesfuge." It is still reasonable to ask writers to imagine for us Satan's phantoms if not Satan himself in any other guise, and to suggest the force of the dark italics, short of propounding them.

Notes

ONE   ADAM'S CURSE

1. W. B. Yeats, *The Poems*, edited by Daniel Albright (London: J. M. Dent and Sons, 1990), pp. 106–7.

2. Samuel Taylor Coleridge, *Table Talk*, edited by Carl Woodring (Princeton: Princeton University Press, 1990), vol. 2, p. 79 (Entry for May 1, 1830).

3. Franz Kafka, *Letters to Milena*, edited by Willy Haas, translated by Tania and James Stern (New York: Schocken Books, 1953), p. 219. Quoted in Gabriel Josipovici, *On Trust: Art and the Temptations of Suspicion* (New Haven: Yale University Press, 1999), pp. 198–199.

4. Soren Kierkegaard, *Either/Or*, vol. 1, translated by David F. Swenson and Lillian Marvin Swenson (Princeton: Princeton University Press, 1959), p. 143. Quoted in Josipovici, *On Trust*, p. 25.

5. Kierkegaard, *Either/Or*, vol. 1, pp. 145–146.

6. Ibid., p. 147.

7. Kierkegaard, *Either/Or*, vol. 2, translated by Walter Lowrie (Princeton: Princeton University Press, 1944), p. 227.

8. *The Variorum Edition of the Poems of W. B. Yeats*, edited by Peter Allt and Russell K. Alspach (New York: Macmillan, corrected third printing, 1966), p. 828.

9. Yeats, *The Poems*, p. 260.

10. Josipovici, *On Trust*, p. 247.

11. Samuel Beckett, *Molloy, Malone Dead, The Unnamable* (London: Calder, 1966, 1994 reprint), p. 334.

12. Yeats, *The Poems*, p. 263.

13. Paul de Man, *Allegories of Reading: Figural Language in Rousseau, Nietzsche, Rilke, and Proust* (New Haven and London: Yale University Press, 1979), p. 10.

14. Ibid., p. 10.

15. John Milton, *Paradise Lost*, edited by Scott Elledge (New York: Norton, 1975), p. 218 (book 10, lines 193–196).

16. Robert Graves, *Complete Poems*, edited by Beryl Graves and Dunstan Ward (Manchester: Carcanet Press, 1995), vol. 1, p. 323.

17. John Locke, *An Essay Concerning Human Understanding*, edited by John W. Yolton (London and New York: Dutton, 1961), vol. 2, p. 105.

18. T. S. Eliot, *Collected Poems 1909–1962* (New York: Harcourt Brace, 1963), p. 204.

19. Paul Valéry, *Degas Manet Morisot*, translated by David Paul (New York: Pantheon, 1964), p. 169.

TWO   GOD WITHOUT THUNDER

1. John Crowe Ransom, *Selected Letters*, edited by Thomas Daniel Young and George Core (Baton Rouge: Louisiana State University Press, 1985), pp. 180–181.

2. Coleridge, *Table Talk*, vol. 1, p. 556.

3. Ransom, *Selected Letters*, p. 181.

4. Allen Tate, *Memories and Essays, Old and New: 1926–1974* (Manchester: Carcanet, 1976), p. 42.

5. John Crowe Ransom, *God without Thunder: An Unorthodox Defense of Orthodoxy* (Hamden, Conn.: Archon Books reprint, 1965), p. 136.

6. Ibid., p. 3.

7. Ibid., p. 40.

8. Ibid., pp. 140–141.

9. Ibid., p. 307.

10. Karl Rahner, *The Trinity*, translated by Joseph Donceel (New York: Seabury Press, 1974), p. 114.

11. Ibid., p. 107.

12. Ibid., p. 110.

13. Ransom, *God without Thunder*, pp. 312–313.

14. Rahner, *The Trinity*, pp. 10–11.

15. Ransom, *God without Thunder*, p. 320.

16. Ibid., pp. 327–328.

17. William Empson, *Milton's God*, rev. ed. (London: Chatto and Windus, 1965), p. 251.

18. Ibid., p. 241.

19. Ibid., p. 243.

20. Ibid., pp. 243–244.

21. Ibid., p. 278.

22. Ibid.

23. Ibid., p. 244.

24. Ibid., p. 245.

25. Ibid., pp. 245–246.

26. Wallace Stevens, *Collected Poems* (New York: Vintage Books, 1990), p. 380.

27. Ibid., p. 381.

28. James Joyce, *A Portrait of the Artist as a Young Man*, edited by Hans Walter Gabler with Walter Hettche (New York: Garland, 1993), p. 137.

29. Herman Melville, *Moby-Dick*, edited by Harrison Hayford and Herschel Parker (New York: Norton, 1967), pp. 50–51.

30. Robert Frost, *Selected Poems* (New York: Holt, Rinehart, and Winston, 1963), pp. 274–275.

31. Ransom, *God without Thunder*, pp. 49–51.

32. *St. Joseph Edition of the New American Bible* (New York: Catholic Book Publishing Co., 1992), p. 570.

33. R. A. F. Mackenzie, "Job," in *The New Jerome Biblical Commentary* (Englewood Clifs, N.J.: Prentice Hall, 1990), p. 488.

34. Ibid., p. 652.

35. Ibid., p. 708.

THREE   CHURCH AND WORLD

1. J. Leslie Houlden, "The Stranger from Heaven," *Times Literary Supplement*, no. 5064, April 21, 2000, p. 3.

2. *The Sermons and Devotional Writings of Gerard Manley Hopkins*, edited by Christopher Devlin (London: Oxford University Press, 1959), p. 37.

3. Emile Durkheim, *The Elementary Forms of the Religious Life: A Study in Religious Sociology*, translated by J. W. Swain (London: Allen and Unwin, 1916), pp. 45, 47.

4. Michael Allen Williams, *Rethinking "Gnosticism"* (Princeton: Princeton University Press, 1999).

5. Elaine Pagels, *The Gnostic Gospels* (New York: Vintage Books, 1979), p. 25.

6. Ibid., pp. 140–141.

7. Paul Johnson, *A History of Christianity* (New York: Atheneum, 1976), p. 76.

8. Henry Adams, *Mont-Saint-Michel and Chartres* (Boston and New York: Houghton Mifflin, 1937 reprint), p. 71.

9. Ibid., p. 1.

10. Ibid., p. 125.

11. Ibid., p. 103.

12. Ibid., p. 162.

13. Ibid., p. 183.

14. Ibid., p. 252.

15. Ibid., p. 276.

16. Ibid., pp. 276–277.

17. Eliot, *Collected Poems 1909–1962*, p. 197.

18. Henry Adams, *The Education of Henry Adams*, edited by Ernest Samuels (Boston: Houghton Mifflin, 1973), p. 383.

19. Adams, *Mont-Saint-Michel and Chartres*, p. 197.

20. Ibid., p. 361.

21. R. P. Blackmur, *A Primer of Ignorance*, edited by Joseph Frank (New York: Harcourt, Brace and World, 1967), p. 248.

22. R. P. Blackmur, *Henry Adams*, edited by Veronica A. Makowsky (New York: Harcourt Brace Jovanovich, 1980), p. 24.

23. Quoted in Johnson, *A History of Christianity*, p. 468.

24. Georg Simmel, *The Philosophy of Money*, translated by Tom Bottomore and David Frisby (London: Routledge and Kegan Paul, 1978), pp. 296–297.

25. Adams, *Mont-Saint-Michel and Chartres*, p. 111.

26. Hans Urs von Balthasar, "Conversion in the New Testament," *Communio*, vol. 1, no. 1 (Spring 1974): 54.

27. Ibid., p. 52.

28. Thomas G. Dalzell, "Lack of Social Drama in Balthasar's Theological Dramatics," *Theological Studies*, vol. 60, no. 3 (September 1999): 3.

29. Hans Urs von Balthasar, *Church and World*, translated by A. V. Littledale with Alexander Dru (New York: Herder and Herder, 1967), p. 143.

30. Hans Urs von Balthasar, "Loneliness in the Church," Explorations in Theology, vol. 4, translated by Edward T. Oakes (San Francisco: Ignatius Press, 1995), pp. 261–298.

31. Hans Urs von Balthasar, "The Fathers, the Scholastics, and Ourselves," *Communio*, vol. 24, no. 2 (Summer 1997): 362.

32. Ibid., p. 363.

33. Ibid., p. 394.

34. Hans Urs von Balthasar, *Prayer* (New York: Paulist Press, 1967), p. 23. Quoted in Rev. James L. Heft, S.M., "Marian Themes in the Writings of Hans Urs von Balthasar," *Marian Studies*, vol. 31 (1980): 55.

35. Eliot, *Collected Poems 1909–1962*, pp. 87–88.

36. Cf. Heft, "Marian Themes," p. 54.

37. John Milbank, *Theology and Social Theory: Beyond Secular Reason* (Oxford: Blackwell, 1998 reprint), p. 407.

38. Ibid., p. 408.

39. Ibid., pp. 433–434.

40. Quoted in Heft, "Marian Themes," p. 57n.

41. Quoted in Robert S. Wistrich, "John Paul II on Jews and Judaism," *Partisan Review*, vol. 67, no. 1 (Winter 2000): 100.

42. Dominic Kirkham, "Letter to the Editor," *Times Literary Supplement*, no. 5050, January 14, 2000, p. 15.

43. John Howard Yoder, "The Anabaptist Dissent: The Logic of the Place of the Disciple in Society," *Concern: A Pamphlet Series for Questions of Christian Renewal*, vol. 1, June 1954, p. 46.

44. Stanley Hauerwas and William Willimon, *Resident Aliens: Life in the Christian Colony* (Nashville: Abingdon Press, 1989). Cf. Alain Epp Weaver, "After Politics: John Howard Yoder, Body Politics, and the Witnessing Church," *Review of Politics*, vol. 61, no. 4 (Fall 1999): 651.

45. Quoted in J. A. Passmore, "Introductory Essay: John Anderson and Twentieth-Century Philosophy," in John Anderson, *Studies in Empirical Philosophy* (Sydney: Angus and Robertson, 1962), p. xxii.

FOUR   OTHERWISE THAN BEING

1. Emmanuel Levinas, *Outside the Subject*, translated by Michael B. Smith (London: Athlone Press, 1993), p. 153.

2. Ibid.

3. Ibid., p. 152.

4. Ibid., p. 3.

5. Levinas, "Comme un consentement à l'horrible," *Le Nouvel Observateur* no. 1211, January 22–28, 1988, p. 48.

6. Ibid.

7. Levinas, *Totality and Infinity*, translated by Alphonso Lingis (Pittsburgh: Duquesne University Press, 1969), p. 134.

8. Ibid., p. 45.

9. *Outside the Subject*, p. 18.

10. *Totality and Infinity*, p. 134.

11. Ibid., p. 46.

12. Levinas, *Otherwise than Being, or, Beyond Essence*, translated by Alphonso Lingis (The Hague: Martinus Nijhoff, 1981), p. 177.

13. Levinas, *Time and the Other*, translated by Richard A. Cohen (Pittsburgh: Duquesne University Press, 1987), p. 41.

14. Levinas, *Collected Philosophical Papers*, translated by Alphonso Lingis (Dordrecht: Martinus Nijhoff,1987), p. 155.

15. *Totality and Infinity*, pp. 21–22.

16. Levinas, *Ethics and Infinity: Conversations with Philippe Nemo*, translated by Richard A. Cohen (Pittsburgh: Duquesne University Press, 1985), p. 75.

17. Ibid., p. 77.

18. *Collected Philosophical Papers*, p. 183.

19. Levinas, *Nine Talmudic Readings*, translated by Annette Aronowicz (Bloomington: Indiana University Press, 1990), p. 99.

20. *Collected Philosophical Papers*, p. 149.

21. Jacques Derrida, *The Gift of Death*, translated by David Wills (Chicago: University of Chicago Press, 1995), pp. 25–26.

22. *Totality and Infinity*, p. 216.

23. Ibid., p. 206.

24. Ibid., p. 39.

25. Ibid., p. 109.

26. Ibid., p. 58.

27. Levinas: "The Trace of the Other," translated by Alphonso Lingis, in Mark C. Taylor, ed., *Deconstruction in Context* (Chicago: University of Chicago Press, 1986), p. 348.

28. *Nine Talmudic Readings*, p. 43.

29. *Outside the Subject*, p. 41.

30. Ibid., p. 45.

31. Levinas, *Autrement qu'être ou au-delà de l'essence*, (The Hague: Martinis Nijhoff, 1974), p. 153.

32. *Outside the Subject*, p. 47.

33. Ibid., p. 23.

34. Levinas, *In the Time of the Nations*, translated by Michael B. Smith (Bloomington: Indiana University Press, 1994), p. 119.

35. Levinas, *Difficult Freedom: Essays on Judaism*, translated by Sean Hand (Baltimore: Johns Hopkins University Press, 1990), pp. 15–16.

36. Ibid., p. 159.

37. *Outside the Subject*, pp. 46–47.

38. Derrida, *The Gift of Death*, p. 84.

39. Quoted in Soloman Malka, *Lire Levinas* (Paris: Editions du Cerf, 1984), p. 81.

40. Jacques Derrida, *Writing and Difference*, translated by Alan Bass (Chicago: University of Chicago Press, 1978), pp. 111 and 133.

41. *Difficult Freedom*, p. 176.

42. Alain Finkielkraut, *The Wisdom of Love*, translated by Kevin O'Neill and David Suchoff (Lincoln and London: University of Nebraska Press, 1997), p. 92.

43. *Outside the Subject*, p. 116.

44. Ibid., p. 118.

45. Ibid., p. 86.

46. *Difficult Freedom*, p. 294.

47. Jurgen Habermas, *The Philosophic Discourse of Modernity*, translated by Frederick Lawrence (MIT Press, 1987), p. 296.

48. Richard Rorty: "Human Rights, Rationality, and Sentimentality," *Yale Review*, vol. 81, no. 4 (October 1993): 18.

49. Levinas, "Reality and its Shadow," *The Levinas Reader*, edited and translated by Sean Hand (Oxford: Blackwell, 1989), p. 133.

50. Ibid., p. 132.

51. Ibid.

52. *Totality and Infinity*, pp. 201–202.

53. *The Levinas Reader*, p. 163.

54. Ibid., p. 165.

55. *Totality and Infinity*, p. 295.

56. J. M. Coetzee, *Age of Iron*, (New York: Random House, 1990).

FIVE   CHRIST AND APOLLO

1. Dante, *Paradiso*, translated by Charles S. Singleton (Princeton: Princeton University Press, 1975), pp. 380–381. Canto 33, lines 142–145: "Here power failed the lofty phantasy; but already my desire and my will were revolved, like a wheel that is evenly moved, by the Love which moves the sun and the other stars."

2. Allen Tate, *Collected Essays* (Denver: Alan Swallow, 1959), p. 431.

3. Ibid., pp. 412–413.

4. Ibid., pp. 434–435.

5. Ibid., p. 414.

6. Ibid., p. 412.

7. Erich Auerbach, *Scenes from the Drama of European Literature* (New York: Meridian Books, 1959), p. 37.

8. William F. Lynch, *Christ and Apollo: The Dimensions of the Literary Imagination* (New York: Sheed and Ward, 1960), p. xiv.

9. Ibid., pp. 154–155.

10. Ibid., p. 164.

11. Ibid., p. 149.

12. Maurice Blondel, *L'Etre et les êtres*, new ed. (Paris: Universitaires de France, 1963), pp. 225–226.

13. E. L. Mascall, *Existence and Analogy: A Sequel to 'He Who Is.'* (London: Longmans, Green, 1949), p. 95.

14. Etienne Gilson, *Le Thomisme*, quoted in Mascall, *Existence and Analogy*, p. 117.

15. Ibid., quoted in Mascall, p. 118.

16. Ibid., p. 120.

17. Quoted in George P. Klubertanz, S.J., *St. Thomas Aquinas on Analogy: A Textual Analysis and Systematic Synthesis* (Chicago: Loyola University Press, 1960), pp. 51–52.

18. William J. Courtenay, "Nominalism and Late Medieval Religion," in Charles Trinkaus and Heiko A. Oberman, eds., *The Pursuit of Holiness in Late Medieval and Renaissance Religion* (Leiden, 1974), p. 39. Quoted in Oakley, note 19.

19. Francis Oakley, "The Absolute and Ordained Power of God in Sixteenth- and Seventeeth-Century Theology," *Journal of the History of Ideas*, vol. 59, no. 3 (April 1998): pp. 442–443.

20. Descartes, Letters to Mersenne, April 15 and May 27, 1630, in *Oeuvres de Descartes*, edited by Charles Adam and Paul Tannery (Paris, 1964–1974), vol. 1, pp. 145, 151–152. Quoted in Francis Oakley, "The Absolute and Ordained Power of God and King in the Sixteenth and Seventeenth Centuries: Philosophy, Science, Politics, and Law," *Journal of the History of Ideas*, vol. 59, no. 4 (October 1998): 672–673.

21. Mary B. Hesse, *Models and Analogies in Science* (London: Sheed and Ward, 1963), p. 95.

22. Lynch, *Christ and Apollo*, p. 153.

23. Quoted in Klubertanz, *St. Thomas Aquinas on Analogy*, p. 30.

24. Shakespeare, *Complete Works*, edited by Hardin Craig and David Bevington (Glenview, Ill.: Scott, Foresman, 1973), pp. 483–484 (Sonnet 73).

25. Robert Frost, *Collected Poems, Prose, and Plays* (New York: Library of America, 1995), p. 206.

26. Hugh Kenner, *The Art of Poetry* (New York: Holt, Rinehart and Winston, 1964), pp. 41–42.

27. *The Complete Poetry of Richard Crashaw*, edited by George Walton Williams (New York: New York University Press, 1972), p. 24.

28. Robert Martin Adams, "Taste and Bad Taste in Metaphysical Poetry," *Hudson Review*, vol. 8 (1955): 67.

29. Roberto Calasso, *The Ruin of Kasch*, translated by William Weaver and Stephen Sartarelli (Cambridge, Mass: Belknap Press of Harvard University Press, 1994), p. 88.

30. Tate, *Collected Essays*, p. 413.

31. Ibid., pp. 413–414.

32. Quoted in Wallace Stevens, "Effects of Analogy," *The Necessary Angel: Essays on Reality and the Imagination* (New York: Knopf, 1951), p. 110.

33. Ibid., pp. 127–128.

34. Ibid., p. 129.

35. Stevens, *Collected Poems*, p. 508.

36. Lynch, *Christ and Apollo*, p. 172.

37. T. S. Eliot, *The Complete Poems and Plays 1909–1950* (New York: Harcourt, Brace and World, 1962), p. 145.

38. Milbank, *Theology and Social Theory*, p. 304.

39. Ibid., p. 296.

40. Ibid., p. 304.

41. Ibid., p. 305.

42. William F. Lynch, *Christ and Prometheus: A New Image of the Secular* (Notre Dame, Ind.: University of Notre Dame Press, 1970), p. 123.

43. Ibid., p.148n.

SIX   BEYOND BELIEF

1. Stevens, *Collected Poems*, p. 336.

2. Robert N. Bellah, *Beyond Belief: Essays on Religion in a Post-Traditional World* (New York: Harper and Row, 1970), p. 203.

3. Stanley Cavell, *Must We Mean What We Say? A Book of Essays* (Cambridge: Cambridge University Press, 1976), pp. 131, 154.

4. Bellah, *Beyond Belief:* p. 197.

5. Karl Marx, Introduction to *Contribution to the Critique of Hegel's Philosophy of Right*, quoted in Cavell, *Must We Mean What We Say?*, p. xxii.

6. T. S. Eliot, "Literature, Science, and Dogma," *The Dial* 82 (March 1927): 241.

7. Ibid., pp. 241–242.

8. Stevens, *Collected Poems*, p. 405.

9. Wallace Stevens, *Opus Posthumous*, edited by Milton J. Bates (New York: Knopf, 1989), p. 189.

10. Ibid., p. 279.

11. Ibid., pp. 259–260.

12. Friedrich Schiller, *Sämtliche Werke*, edited by G. Fricke and H. G. Göpfort (Munich, 1965), vol. 1, p. 169: "Da die Götter menschlicher noch waren/ Waren Menschen göttlicher."

13. Bellah, *Beyond Belief:* p. 242.

14. Ibid., p. 227.

15. Ibid., p. 221.

16. Ibid., p. 12.

17. Ibid., p. 16.

18. Ibid., p. 21.

19. Robert N. Bellah, *The Broken Covenant: American Civil Religion in Time of Trial*, 2d ed. (Chicago: University of Chicago Press, 1992), p. xii.

20. Alexis de Tocqueville, *Democracy in America*, vol. 1 (Garden City, N.Y.: Doubleday, Anchor Books, 1954), p. 311. Quoted in Bellah, *Beyond Belief*, p. 180.

21. Quoted in Bellah, *Beyond Belief*, pp. 168–169.

22. Bellah, *Beyond Belief*, p. 170.

23. Robert N. Bellah et al., *Habits of the Heart: Individualism and Commitment in American Life* (Berkeley: University of California Press, 1985), p. 225.

24. Cf. Milbank, *Theology and Social Theory*, p. 321.

25. Paul Valéry, *Analects*, translated by Stuart Gilbert (Princeton: Princeton University Press, 1970), p. 183. Quoted in T. W. Adorno, *Notes to Literature*, edited by Rolf Tiedemann, translated by Shierry Weber Nicholson (New York: Columbia University Press, 1991), vol. 1, p. 139.

26. David Walsh, *The Growth of the Liberal Soul* (Columbia and London: University of Missouri Press, 1997), pp. 199–201.

SEVEN   AFTER VIRTUE

1. Alasdair MacIntyre, *After Virtue: A Study in Moral Theory*, 2d ed. (Notre Dame, Ind.: University of Notre Dame Press, 1984), pp. 110–111.

2. Ibid., p. 226.

3. Ibid., p. 10.

4. Ibid., p. 252.

5. Ibid.

6. Ibid., pp. 11–12.

7. Philip Larkin, *Collected Poems*, ed. Anthony Thwaite (London: Marvell Press and Faber and Faber, 1988), pp. 208–209.

8. Czeslaw Milosz, "The Real and the Paradigms," *Poetry Australia* 72 (October 1979): 62–63.

9. Larkin, *Collected Poems*, p. 98.

10. William Empson, *Collected Poems* (New York: Harcourt, Brace, 1949), pp. 58–59.

11. Seamus Heaney, *The Redress of Poetry* (New York: Farrar, Straus and Giroux, 1995), p. 149.

12. Ibid., pp. 159–160.

13. Richard Rorty, "The Inspirational Value of Great Works of Literature," *Raritan*, vol. 16, no. 1 (Summer 1996): 15.

14. F. R. Leavis, *Valuation in Criticism and Other Essays*, edited by G. Singh (Cambridge: Cambridge University Press, 1986), p. 281.

15. Ibid.

16. Ibid., p. 288.

17. Ibid., pp. 277–278.

18. Ibid., p. 288.

19. Of the several versions of "The Ruined Cottage," I quote the one that became the first book of *The Excursion*. William Wordsworth, *The Poems*, edited by John O. Hayden (New Haven: Yale University Press, 1977), vol. 2, p. 57 (line 604).

20. F. R. Leavis, *The Critic as Anti-Philosopher*, edited by G. Singh (Athens: University of Georgia Press, 1983), p. 35

21. MacIntyre, *After Virtue*, p. 259.

22. William Empson, *Seven Types of Ambiguity* (London: Chatto and Windus, 1930), p. 247.

23. William Empson, *The Structure of Complex Words* (London: Chatto and Windus, 1951), p. 158.

24. Geoffrey Hill, *The Lords of Limit: Essays on Literature and Ideas* (New York: Oxford University Press, 1984), p. 94.

EIGHT   THE DEATH OF SATAN

1. J. F. Powers, *Prince of Darkness and Other Stories* (Garden City, N.Y.: Image Books, 1958), pp. 190–191.

2. Henry James, *The Art of the Novel: Critical Prefaces*, with an introduction by R. P. Blackmur (New York: Scribner, 1962 reprint), p. 176.

3. Ibid., p. 177.

4. Powers, *Prince of Darkness*, p. 193.

5. Percy Bysshe Shelley, *Complete Works: Prose: Volume VII*, edited by Roger Ingpen and Walter E. Peck (London: Julian Editions, Ernest Benn Ltd., 1930), p. 92.

6. Ibid., pp. 90–91.

7. Paul Ricoeur, *The Symbolism of Evil*, translated by Emerson Buchanan (New York: Harper and Row, 1967), p. 315.

8. Quoted in Elledge, *Paradise Lost: An Authoritative Text, Backgrounds and Sources, Criticism*, pp. 290–291.

9. John Milton, *Works*, edited by Frank Allen Patterson et al. (New York: Columbia University Press, 1933), p. 67.

10. Ibid., p. 73.

11. Ibid., p. 69.

12. Ibid., p. 115.

13. Quoted in Elledge, *Paradise Lost*, p. 287. Milton added to the citation from Lactantius the comment: ". . . although even these reasons are not satisfactory."

14. Ibid., 5.116–119, p. 107.

15. Frank Kermode, "Adam Unparadised," in Kermode, ed., *The Living Milton* (New York: Macmillan, 1961), p. 99.

16. Quoted in Elledge, *Paradise Lost*, p. 291.

17. Sainte-Beuve, "Le Cahier vert," in *Cahiers* (Paris: Gallimard, 1973), vol. 1, pp. 119–120. Quoted in Roberto Calasso, *The Ruin of Kasch*, p. 92.

18. Kermode, "Adam Unparadised," p. 106.

19. T. S. Eliot, *Selected Essays* (London: Faber and Faber, 1963 reprint), p. 429.

20. Baudelaire, *Correspondance*, edited by Claude Pichois and Jean Ziegler (Paris: Gallimard, 1973), vol. 2, p. 53. Quoted in Jonathan Culler, "Baudelaire's Satanic Verses," *Diacritics*, vol. 28, no. 3 (1998): 99.

21. Baudelaire, *Oeuvres complètes*, edited by Claude Pichois (Paris: Gallimard, 1975), vol. 2, p. 68. Quoted in Culler, "Baudelaire's Satanic Verses," p. 99.

22. Baudelaire, *Oeuvres complètes*, vol. 2, p. 68. Quoted in Culler, p. 98.

23. Culler, "Baudelaire's Satanic Verses," p. 99.

24. Emerson, *Selected Writings*, edited by Brooks Atkinson (New York: Modern Library, 1950), p. 359.

25. Eliot, *Collected Poems 1909–1962*, p. 204.

26. Frank Kermode, *Wallace Stevens* (Edinburgh: Oliver and Boyd, 1960), p. 103.

27. Stevens, *Collected Poems*, p. 315.

28. Wallace Stevens, "The Course of a Particular," in *Opus Posthumous*, p. 124.

29. Andrew Delbanco, *The Death of Satan* (New York: Farrar, Straus and Giroux, 1995), p. 58.

30. Milbank, *Theology and Social Theory*, pp. 124–125, and Kenneth Surin, *Theology and the Problem of Evil* (Oxford: Blackwell, 1986), pp. 1–58.

31. Immanuel Kant, *Religion within the Limits of Reason Alone*, translated by T. M. Greene and H. H. Hudson (New York: Harper Torchbooks, 1960), pp. 28, 32.

32. Ricoeur, *The Symbolism of Evil*, p. 273.

33. André Gide, *The Counterfeiters*, translated by Dorothy Bussy (New York: Knopf, 1951 reprint), p. 202. André Gide, *Romans* (Paris: Librairie Gallimard, 1958), p. 1109. English translation modified.

34. Gide, *The Counterfeiters*, pp. 364–365. *Les Faux-monnayeurs*, in *Romans*, p. 1247.

35. Gide, *The Counterfeiters*, p. 365. *Les Faux-monnayeurs*, pp. 1247–1248. English translation modified.

36. Blackmur, *A Primer of Ignorance*, p. 31.

37. Finkielkraut, *The Wisdom of Love*, p. 70.

38. P. C. Vey, "Cartoon," *New Yorker*, August 23 and 30, 1999, p. 186.

39. Wallace Shawn, "On the Context of the Play," *Aunt Dan and Lemon* (New York: Grove Press, 1985), p. 99.

40. George Steiner, *Language and Silence* (New York: Atheneum, 1967), p. 150.

41. Robert Boyers, *Atrocity and Amnesia: The Political Novel since 1945* (New York: Oxford University Press, 1985), p. 172.

42. Jean Baudrillard, *The Transparency of Evil: Essays on Extreme Phenomena*, translated by James Benedict (London: Verso, 1993), p. 81.

43. Ibid., p. 149.

44. Walter Benjamin, *The Origin of German Tragic Drama*, translated by John Osborne (London: NLB, 1977), p. 178.

45. Shakespeare, *Complete Works*, p. 1016.

INDEX